bad
cheerleader

also by ALEX THAYER
Happy & Sad & Everything True

bad cheerleader

ALEX THAYER

aladdin
NEW YORK   AMSTERDAM/ANTWERP   LONDON
TORONTO   SYDNEY/MELBOURNE   NEW DELHI

This book is a work of fiction. Any references to historical events, real people, or real places are used fictitiously. Other names, characters, places, and events are products of the author's imagination, and any resemblance to actual events or places or persons, living or dead, is entirely coincidental.

ALADDIN
An imprint of Simon & Schuster Children's Publishing Division
1230 Avenue of the Americas, New York, New York 10020
For more than 100 years, Simon & Schuster has championed authors and the stories they create. By respecting the copyright of an author's intellectual property, you enable Simon & Schuster and the author to continue publishing exceptional books for years to come. We thank you for supporting the author's copyright by purchasing an authorized edition of this book.
No amount of this book may be reproduced or stored in any format, nor may it be uploaded to any website, database, language-learning model, or other repository, retrieval, or artificial intelligence system without express permission. All rights reserved. Inquiries may be directed to Simon & Schuster, 1230 Avenue of the Americas, New York, NY 10020 or permissions@simonandschuster.com.
First Aladdin hardcover edition November 2025
Text © 2025 by Alex Thayer
Cover illustration © 2025 by Carmen Martínez
Also available in an Aladdin paperback edition.
All rights reserved, including the right of reproduction in whole or in part in any form.
ALADDIN and related logo are registered trademarks of Simon & Schuster, LLC.
For information about special discounts for bulk purchases, please contact Simon & Schuster Special Sales at 1-866-506-1949 or business@simonandschuster.com.
Simon & Schuster strongly believes in freedom of expression and stands against censorship in all its forms. For more information, visit BooksBelong.com.
The Simon & Schuster Speakers Bureau can bring authors to your live event. For more information or to book an event, contact the Simon & Schuster Speakers Bureau at 1-866-248-3049 or visit our website at www.simonspeakers.com.
Book design by Heather Palisi
The text of this book was set in Calisto.
Manufactured in the United States of America 1025 BVG
10 9 8 7 6 5 4 3 2 1
Library of Congress Cataloging-in-Publication Data
Names: Thayer, Alex author
Title: Bad cheerleader / Alex Thayer.
Description: New York : Aladdin, 2025. | Audience term: Preteens | Audience: Ages 10 and Up | Summary: "A dyslexic bookworm joins her school's cheerleading squad to investigate her sister's strange behavior in this insightful and sharp middle grade novel about the unbreakable bonds of sisterhood. Seventh grader Bag loves to read. It doesn't come easy to her, thanks to her dyslexia, but she's determined, and she spends every afternoon after school at the library. It's a ritual she refuses to miss. Then a new career opportunity for her mother means Bag will no longer have a ride to her cherished library. Instead, Bag will have to wait for a ride at school. With her sister, Minerva. At cheerleading practice. Bag is uncoordinated and completely uninterested in school spirit. But she is curious about what her sister has been hiding. Minerva has been acting stranger than usual, and Bag has been noticing. So while cheerleading practice may be the last place Bag wants to be, she's going to use her time wisely and get to the bottom of Minerva's secrets"—Provided by publisher.
Identifiers: LCCN 2025003826 (print) | LCCN 2025003827 (ebook) | ISBN 9781665955270 hardcover | ISBN 9781665955287 paperback | ISBN 9781665955294 ebook
Subjects: CYAC: Sisters—Fiction | Dyslexia—Fiction | Cheerleading—Fiction | Middle schools—Fiction | Schools—Fiction | LCGFT: Fiction | Novels
Classification: LCC PZ7.1.T447357 Bad 2025 (print) | LCC PZ7.1.T447357 (ebook) | DDC [Fic]—dc23 /eng/20250320
LC record available at https://lccn.loc.gov/2025003826
LC ebook record available at https://lccn.loc.gov/2025003827

for miranda

bad
cheerleader

chapter one

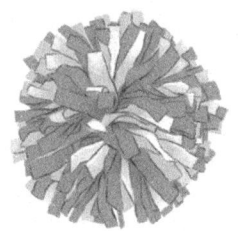

THE FIRST LINES OF BOOKS ARE SO PHONY. IT'S like they trick the reader into reading the whole book with one sparkling good sentence. Truth is, the beginning of a book doesn't make a book great. It's the ending that matters most. Which is why I read the last page before I read the beginning. Because if there's one thing I hate most in the world, it's surprises.

I've already had too many surprises. Like when we had to move from Manhattan to Rhode Island. Or when my cat, Rascal, ate rat poison and died. Or when my mom took my sister to Ryan's Arcade and not me. Or when my dad left without saying goodbye.

I don't want any more surprises.

This morning is no different.

I crack open the end of *The Old Man and the Sea*, my

newest book from the library. I can't wait to get started. I've got twenty-three minutes before we leave for school.

Knuckles knock against my bedroom door, and Minerva says my name. "Bag."

I ignore her and focus on the last page. ". . . looking down in the water among the empty beer cans and dead barracudas a woman saw . . ."

"Bag," she says again.

Old hinges bend and squeak as she opens my bedroom door.

My eyes stay on the book. "Leave."

"Mom wants to talk to us," she says.

I grunt and glare at my sister. It's School Spirit Day, and she certainly plays the part: flat-ironed hair, skinny lips, curvy hips, and an unwrinkled cheerleading uniform. Only, this morning I see something different about her polyester skirt. I notice a small burn hole near the hem, no bigger than a pea.

"Girls!" Mom shouts.

"See, Bag," Minerva says. "Told you."

"Fine." I tuck *The Old Man and the Sea* under my arm and follow my sister down the hallway.

Random Thought 929.4

My real name is Margaret. When I was little, back when my dad was around, he started calling me Maggie. Minerva quickly changed "Maggie" to "Baggie." Then somewhere along the line "Baggie" got shortened to "Bag." When we first moved here, I thought about using "Maggie" again, but then that would remind me of my dad and our old life in New York. So I told everyone my name is "Bag." Here's what I've learned about names: Once they stick, they stick for a really long time.

The kitchen is the same as always. A disaster.

Next to the sink there's a bowl of garbanzo beans, on the counter there's oodles of pita triangles, and the kitchen table is covered with juice boxes, packets of olives, and cheese squares. Mom is, once again, running late. Every morning she makes lunches to sell at private schools in Providence. Every morning she barely finishes.

Mom chops cherry tomatoes on a wooden cutting board, which is resting on top of the oven. She hacks into the tomatoes, while I check to make sure the oven is off. (It is.) Then I look at her face, expecting to see her usual frown. But today Mom smiles a huge, happy grin.

"Do you need help?" I ask.

"Mom," Minerva cuts in. "How are you this far behind?"

"Just about to make the hummus!" Mom leaves the

tomatoes on the cutting board and moves to the garbanzo beans on the counter. "Mediterranean Medleys," she says. "They'll be done in a jiffy!"

I clutch my book as Minerva groans and says to me, "Are you seriously wearing that? On School Spirit Day? It's so rude."

"School Sprit Day is an optional activity." I look down at my favorite tee, a Salvation Army find with soft white cotton and big black letters that say I DON'T PLAY SPORTS. It's totally something my dad would wear. Like me, he loves an ironic T-shirt. On the other hand, Mom and Minerva do not like ironic T-shirts. They prefer skirts and dresses and fancy low-cut tops that show off their curves.

"You can borrow something from my closet," Mom says to me. "I've got a light blue sweater that would look great on you."

"No thanks," I say.

"Big mistake." Minerva won't look at me, as if the sight of me in the T-shirt is already causing her embarrassment. Mom sighs.

Obviously my mom and my sister will never understand the charm of my T-shirt.

I plop down at the kitchen table. That's when I notice Mom's headshot under a pile of cheese squares. Her bright white smile pops out like a high-beam flashlight. Seeing the picture surprises me. I didn't know she still kept them. Mom hasn't acted in years, not since her soap was canceled. I stare at the photo, and a shudder runs up my neck. The headshot is completely out of place, kind of like the burn that's on the hem of Minerva's skirt.

> **Random Thought 790.2**
> Mom's soap was called *The Rich and the Radiant*. She was one of the stars, but there were lots of stars, and maybe that's the problem with soaps: too many people all in the same place, all at the same time, all needing to feel like the most important.

"Minerva," Mom says. "Can you put the tomatoes into Tupperware?"

At the sound of her name, Minerva jumps to action. It's weird. My sister never helps. Usually she's too busy ironing her cheerleading uniform or brushing her hair until it shines like a stick of melted butter. Minerva uses the elastic band she keeps on her wrist and ties her long hair into a ponytail. Why is she so eager?

"Just a scoop," Mom tells her. "Bag, you can put the cheese into the crate?"

I set down *The Old Man and the Sea*. I'm so far behind. I read my two previous library books, *Ask the Dust* and *The Catcher in the Rye*, in record time. I look at *The Old*

Man and the Sea longingly. Then I toss the cheese squares into the large crate that's on the floor. There's no way I'll be able to read the last page before school. I grind my teeth together knowing this cheese job is setting my reading schedule even further behind.

I wish Ridgley were here. He could give a performance of *The Old Man and the Sea* and read it out loud while I pack the cheese. Ridgley is a *thespian*. At least that's what he calls it. Before I met Ridgley, I thought the word was "actor," but Ridgley says "thespian" sounds way more interesting.

I toss another cheese square into the crate and smile thinking about Ridgley being here, reading to me. But it's a silly thought. He's never come to my house before, even though I'd like him to.

With each cheese square I pick up, I see more and more of Mom's old headshot. Her chin, her ears, her nose, her blond hair that looks just like Minerva's, her unwrinkled forehead that now has wrinkles, her long fingers, her eyes. Her hazel eyes that have more gray than green and remind me of a forest at night.

"Is this the right-size scoop?" Minerva holds up a spoonful of diced tomatoes. Her diction is perfect. Her tomatoes are perfect. Her impromptu ponytail is perfect.

"Looks good," Mom says without really looking.

Minerva places the diced tomatoes into the Tupperware container. At the same time, Mom plops down a gob of hummus and tosses in a piece of pita. They work side by side as Mom says, "Now, girls, there's something I'd like to talk to you about."

Oh great. Whenever Mom begins a sentence with "Now, girls, there's something I'd like to talk to you about," she doesn't want to talk about anything. She wants to tell us something, and the thing she wants to tell us is bad.

Like when her soap was canceled and we had to move from Manhattan to Rhode Island because our apartment was too expensive, or when we completely ran out of money and she stopped auditioning and started making school lunches, or when she told Dad he had to move out, or when the doctor told her I was dyslexic and I needed special help with reading.

I toss a few juice boxes into the crate even though Mom didn't ask me to. They need to be loaded, and I'm not looking forward to what she's about to tell us, so I figure I'll feel better if I'm only half listening.

"I booked a job," Mom says.

"A job. Huh. Well, that's not so bad." I toss more juice boxes into the crate.

"Not so bad?" she says. "It's great!"

"What new school are you delivering to?" I ask.

"Not that kind of job," Mom replies.

Oh no. I glance at her headshot. Oh no. Oh no. Oh no.

"A lead role!" Mom cries. "It's a great role. There's this memoir that came out a while ago. Have you heard of it? *The Glass Castle*. The parents are homeless, and they're adapting the book for the stage, and I got the part. I got the part of the homeless mother!"

"The homeless mother?" I look at Mom's beautiful headshot, which is as far from looking homeless as a person could get.

Then I look at Mom scooping blobs of hummus. She's got her frizzy morning hair, and she's wearing a fleece bathrobe. Her headshot and her real self barely look like the same person. Mom squeezes Minerva's arm. "Aren't you girls excited?"

I don't respond because I'm not excited. After Mom's soap ended, she started auditioning for off-Broadway plays in New York. It was terrible. Either she wouldn't get the part or she would get the part, she'd start rehearsals, and she'd be really upset with the production of the play. It was a lose-lose situation. I don't want her to get her hopes up again.

Minerva's mouth turns down, like she's thinking the same thing. "I didn't know you were auditioning."

Mom goes back to plopping gobs of hummus into the Tupperware containers. "My ex-agent called and said it was the part of a lifetime. I mean, it's not Broadway or anything. The play's at the Center Stage Theater."

"Center what?" Minerva asks.

"The Center Stage Theater. It's in Providence." Mom chucks her hummus spoon into the sink. "God, wouldn't it be great if this part got us back to New York?"

I pick up Mom's headshot. "The part of a homeless person?"

"It's a wonderful role," Mom tells me.

I'm holding the headshot with a clenched fist. The photo wrinkles in my grip. I drop it onto the table because I don't want to get in trouble for ruining her face. I look to see if Mom sees, but she's focused on the Mediterranean Medleys. She puts more pita triangles into the Tupperware containers and sort of looks like a normal mom even though I know she isn't.

I don't want to watch, so I stare at the kitchen wall instead. It's covered with Mom's handwriting. The notes started last year. She writes them directly on the wall. I find the first note she wrote next to the light switch. *Bag's birthday.* I think she wrote the note to remember to get cake and wrap presents, which was nice. But it's not her only note. My eyes move to the note about the dentist, the note to get a wax, the note about a delivery. Her handwriting is messy. *Bake sale brownies,* I think one says? My eyes move to the wall next to the fridge. *Bottle recycling. Vendor drop.* On the wall near the sink she wrote, *Insurance card.* Above the toaster, a new note:

Call Tom

My eyes stay stuck on the loopy letters. *Call Tom.*

I didn't notice that one before. When did she write it? Did she call him? What did he say? Does he want to come home? Does he know about her play? Does he miss us? Does he miss me? I stare at the name as if it could belong to anyone, when really the name belongs to him. My dad.

"Do you have to take the part?" Minerva asks.

"I already did," Mom says.

"Without talking to us?" Minerva places a scoop of tomato into the Tupperware, and a speck splashes up and hits the arm of her cheerleading uniform. "Ugh," she moans.

"It's not like I signed a contract." Mom slaps the lids onto the Tupperware while Minerva rushes to the sink and wets the sleeve of her shirt.

At the same time, I start chucking the juice boxes into the crate again. They slam on top of each other, and I feel a tiny bit better.

"Look," Mom says. "Opening night is a month from now, which is going to be so exciting, but rehearsal times are tricky. Rehearsals are weekday afternoons. I won't be able to pick you up after school."

"What do I care?" Minerva says from the sink. "I have cheerleading."

"Hold on," I say. "What about the library?"

"Well . . ." Mom turns to me. Her forehead wrinkles,

and her hazel eyes peer into mine. "I was wondering if you could go to the library at school?"

"The library at school is only open during the school day."

She rubs her forehead and gets a smudge of hummus on her brow.

"Mom, I need you to drive me to the public library. It's where I do my best reading."

"Sweetheart, I won't have time."

"I'll walk."

"Don't be silly. The public library is miles away."

My heart beats inside my throat.

"It's only a month," Mom explains. "After opening night the shows will be in the evenings. Then I can drive you." She leans her butt against the counter. "It's been such a hard year, and this is good news. This is really good news for us."

I want to tell her that the play isn't good news for us. It isn't good news for her. I want to remind her of the off-Broadway shows. I want to tell her this, but I don't want to make her mad.

So I stare at the messy writing that covers our kitchen walls. *Bag's teacher conference. Snow tires.* The more I stare, the more the walls seem to cave in around me. The room grows smaller as I pull my T-shirt away from my neck. *Rent.* I see how much she does for us. I also see the enormous mess she's made of our kitchen. "Why not use

Post-its?" I motion to the mess of a wall. "I've told you this before, Mom. Post-its make everything organized."

"Oh, I guess it's easier this way. Really all I need to do is write myself reminders, and then I never look again. It's the writing that helps me remember."

"That doesn't explain why you don't use paper," I say. "Or a dry-erase board."

Mom stacks more Tupperware boxes in the crate. Then she throws her hands up in the air. "You know what, there's a lot to be said for creative expression, Baggie. Get out of your head and into your body!"

"Isn't my head part of my body?" I ask.

Mom claps her hands together as if she's scooping up a good idea. "Maybe you could join cheerleading with Minerva," she says. "That would shake things up!"

"Absolutely not," I say.

Minerva begins to laugh. She laughs hard, bends over, and clutches her stomach. "Bag as a cheerleader!" she cries. "Stop it! I'm going to pee my pants!"

I narrow my eyes at her. "Like that time in New York when Mom had to bring an extra pair of shorts to school?"

"You little . . ." Minerva lunges at me, but I dodge out of the way.

"Minerva. Bag." Mom puts the last Tupperware box into the crate. "That's enough. Come on, girls. Let's get this food into the truck."

"I'm not going to cheerleading," I say to Mom. "I'll find somewhere to read at school. You can pick me up after your rehearsal."

"Sounds good." Mom hefts the large crate into her arms.

My sister doesn't say another word.

She picks up a crate and pretends like everything is fine, when the truth is, we couldn't be further away from fine.

Random Thought 177.3
Minerva looks good on the outside,
but on the inside she's all mixed up.
Like, when Dad left, she didn't cry
or anything. She went on acting like
everything was the same. Here's what I
know about my sister: She's the perfect
first line of a book, and the rest of her
doesn't make any sense.

chapter two

THE NEWPORT BRIDGE LOOMS BEFORE US. ITS pale green paint reminds me of moss. The steel pylons remind me of elephant legs. The arched middle reminds me of an upside-down heart. I love the bridge.

Mom takes a left at the light and drives under the overpass. At the same time, I lean forward, hoping to hear the soft echo of waves bouncing against the bridge's giant pylons.

"It's freezing in here!"

Minerva speaks as if we're sitting miles apart. We aren't. I'm sitting next to her. We're less than an inch away from each other. Mom is on the other side of me. I'm stuck in the middle seat of the truck, not by choice.

Minerva turns the heater to full blast. I sink in my seat, wishing for a breath of fresh air, wishing I had the window seat. I shove my face down near my lap, but the hot air is unavoidable. It blows at us from the vents, full speed ahead.

Speaking of full speed ahead, Mom banks a right at the rotary, and her bony elbow jabs into my ribs. Even worse, Minerva's hips slide over to my area and press against my upper leg.

I ask, "Can someone roll down a window?"

"No," Minerva says.

"We're almost there," Mom says. "Hold tight."

"Hold tight?" I moan. "I'm in the worst seat and I'm hot and I'm going to throw up."

"Oh, Bag," Mom says.

She doesn't say anything else. She doesn't make Minerva roll down her window. She doesn't roll down her own window. I wish Dad were here. Like me, he prefers driving with the windows open.

Two and a half miserable minutes later, Mom stops the truck in front of school, and I readjust my glasses. Of course, I don't *need* the glasses. No one knows except my mom.

It happened last year, in sixth grade, back when we were living in New York. My teacher, Ms. Viola, said the class was going to read a book out loud.

She called on the person sitting in front of me. Then she called on the person next to me. Then she called on me. I could read the paragraph, but I knew it would take a long time, and I didn't want my voice to quiver in front of everyone.

So I said, "I can't."

"Of course you can."

"I can't."

"Stop kidding around."

"I'm not kidding."

Ms. Viola called my mom, probably to get me in trouble. But Mom wasn't mad. She was worried. Mom brought me to the doctor because she thought I needed glasses. Turns out it was dyslexia.

"Dyslexia," the doctor said.

Mom replied, "Are you sure? My daughter loves books."

"Yes," he told her. "I'm certain."

Mom shook her head. "Unbelievable."

"Can I still get glasses?" I asked.

"Baggie," Mom said, "you don't need them. Your eyes are fine."

My eyes may have been fine, but obviously my brain was a whole other story.

"I—"

I wanted to say, *I need glasses to look smart.* Because I knew I wasn't.

Even though I didn't finish the sentence, Mom must've known what I was thinking. That day she bought me plain-glass glasses. I've worn them ever since.

Random Thought 612.8
Maybe that's something everyone needs, not necessarily glasses but a way to express the outside in a way that feels true to the inside.

"See you at four. I'll meet you right here. In front of school." Mom looks at me. Now her hazel eyes look completely green, super green, like a pine forest sparkling in morning sunlight.

"Pick me up at the gym," Minerva says. She pushes the truck door open and wraps her arms around herself. "It's too cold to wait outside. Cheerleading ends at four."

"Okay," Mom says. "Bag, you can meet us at the gym too."

"Sure, Mom. No problem."

After Minerva hops down, she turns to face me, standing next to the open door of the truck. "I don't want you in the gym."

"I'm not going to be in the gym," I say. "I'm meeting Mom in front of the gym."

"I don't want you near the gym," Minerva says again. "Period."

"Stop telling me what to do," I say.

"Girls," Mom says. "I don't have time for the drama."

Mom's sitting next to me in the cab of the truck. Her Lunches by Lenore are stacked in back. I imagine that the cold air is freezing the hummus into solid little bricks.

"Do not go near that gym," Minerva tells me.

Seriously. Why is she being so mean? It's not like she's ever nice to me, but this morning she's over-the-top. Normally she acts annoyed with me. But today it's like she downright hates me. I mean, there's no reason for her to be this upset with me. Why is she freaking out? Maybe, just maybe, there's something more than me that Minerva's upset about?

A car honks behind us, urging Mom to get moving. They just dropped off a kid, a fifth grader, and he's already walking into school.

"Baggie, where should I pick you up?" Mom says quickly.

Minerva waits, making sure I don't tell Mom to pick me up at the gym. I sigh. "Fine. I'll meet you here, in front of school, after you get . . ." I narrow my eyes at my sister. "Minerva."

I hop out of the truck, and Minerva narrows her eyes back at me.

"Sounds good, girls! See you at four! Wish me luck at my first rehearsal!" Mom taps her horn and then speeds away.

Minerva pinches my upper arm. "You'd better not go to the gym."

I push her away from me. "Why are you making such a big deal about it?"

Without responding she scurries toward the front entrance of Thompson Middle. Even though we've got seventeen minutes until the bell rings, Minerva rushes as if she were late. She doesn't bother to zip her coat. Her typically organized backpack is stuffed with papers that stick out from the top. Her cheerleading skirt still has that tiny burn hole.

I give my fake glasses a final adjustment before I head to school. Then, as I walk toward the brick building, I rub the spot on my arm where Minerva pinched me.

Something's going on with my sister. I can feel it.

chapter three

ENGLISH IS MY FAVORITE CLASS FOR THREE REASONS: one, the reading; two, the writing; and three, Mr. Perkins. Mr. Perkins keeps a quiet room, speaks with a gentle voice, and smells musty, like a stack of old books.

I walk into English and sigh. The room feels like a hug. I take my seat in the front row and almost forget about Minerva until a cheerleading uniform lands next to me. The uniform belongs to Mimi Fookwire. I look down at my T-shirt that says I DON'T PLAY SPORTS. My ironic tee is the opposite of Mimi Fookwire and her perfect, unwrinkled cheerleading uniform which matches Minerva's.

"So," Mr. Perkins begins, "we're going to shake things up today."

He wears a dark green T-shirt with a few cat hairs

stuck to the collar. I imagine Mr. Perkins's cat is a calico and somewhat cranky. I imagine Mr. Perkins sits on a comfy sofa, reading something very complicated, like *The Canterbury Tales* or *Beowulf*, or some other interesting book with really tricky words, while patting his calico cat.

"Poetry," Mr. Perkins says, and breaks me away from my thoughts about him. "Today we're going to talk about poetry. What makes words poetic? What makes words sound like poetry, feel like poetry . . . ?"

Mimi Fookwire raises her hand. Mimi is always raising her hand. We have English and math together and she's constantly raising her hand.

"Yes?" Mr. Perkins says.

"I like the poetry of Sharon Creech," she replies.

The name Sharon Creech swirls around in my head. I picture her books: *Love That Dog, Saving Winslow, Hate That Cat, Moo.* . . . I picture where the books are shelved in the Newport Public Library. . . .

"I love Sharon Creech!" I say before I have time to stop myself. "But she's not a poet. Her books are in the middle-grade fiction section of the library. *Love That Dog* is my absolute favorite!"

I lean back in my seat and wait for Mr. Perkins to compliment me on my knowledge of books. He doesn't.

Instead he looks at Mimi and says, "I couldn't agree more, Mimi. Sharon Creech is a wonderful writer, and her books are very poetic. In fact, I'm pretty sure Ms. Creech refers to herself as a poet." Mr. Perkins looks at me, then says to everyone, "Let's all remember to raise our hands in class when we'd like to speak."

The air moves out of my body like I've turned into one of those awful whoopee cushions and someone just sat on me. I've been flattened and squished like a crummy piece of plastic. I scan the room for Ridgley. He sits two seats behind me. I glance at his white T-shirt, which is just like mine, minus the words.

"Don't worry," Ridgley mouths.

I frown, like I totally messed up. "I should've raised my hand," I mouth back.

Mr. Perkins interrupts our moment. "Bag," he says.

I whip around to face him.

"Is there another book of poetry you like?" he asks.

"Um." Of course there are poetry books I like. I have a long list of them, but when I open my mouth, I can't think of a single title.

"Um," I say again.

"Oh, that's all right," Mr. Perkins says. "If you think of one, please let us know. As for the rest of you . . ." Mr. Perkins rubs his chin. "Whatcha got?"

Hands shoot into the air. I hear *Brown Girl Dreaming*, *The Crossover*, *Rhyme Schemer*, and *House Arrest*.

I've read all those books. Why couldn't I think of the titles? For a moment I worry I have amnesia or some hidden brain tumor, but then I realize it's the dyslexia. It's been a long time since the words in my brain wouldn't connect to my mouth, but every once in a while it creeps up on me.

The class continues to talk about poetry, and Mr. Perkins gets more and more excited. I'm not even part of the discussion. I try to get Ridgley's attention, but he doesn't see me because he's got his own hand up in the air. I look over at Mimi and she glares at me, probably because I interrupted her.

Random Thought 153.2
I'm dumber than dumb.

The day keeps getting worse.

During geography my favorite pencil breaks. During Spanish I botch saying "Me llamo Bag." During science I can't find my notebook. I still haven't read the ending of *The Old Man and the Sea*. And Minerva keeps glaring at me every time we pass each other in the hall. Then Minerva rolls her eyes at me when we end up beside each other on our way to the cafeteria. Unfortunately, the seventh graders (me) and the eighth graders (Minerva) eat lunch at the same time.

I follow behind Minerva and her posse of cheerleaders: Emily S., Emily C., and Mimi. They gather around my sister like bees swarming their queen. Each girl wears a cheerleading uniform for School Spirit Day. Like bees, their uniforms look the same. Almost everything about them looks the same. Their long hair, their uniforms, their perfectly white sneakers.

The only differences: Mimi is a foot shorter than Emily S., Emily C., and Minerva. Mimi is in seventh grade (like me), while Minerva, Emily C., and Emily S. are in eighth. And, of course, Minerva has blond hair. The other girls have brown hair. Other than that, the cheerleaders are exactly the same.

As they enter the cafeteria, Minerva doesn't hold the swinging door for me, and I jut my arm out just in time to stop it from crashing into my shoulder. Then I stumble inside.

The cafeteria smells like beef jerky and dirty feet. I quickly move to my regular seat, the seat near the window, the seat farthest away from the stinky hot-lunch line. As I walk, I hear the clinking of silverware against plastic trays, the opening and closing of ziplock baggies, the setting down of cups, the crinkling of tinfoil, the shuffling of chairs. The sounds of the cafeteria mix like music.

When I get to my spot, I pull out my Mediterranean Medley. Under the lid I've got tomatoes, hummus, pita triangles, and cheese squares. I also pull out a juice box. But oh no, oh no, oh no. The juice box is empty.

I shove my hand into my backpack, and the bottom is wet. Faster than fast I dump the contents and find

The Old Man and the Sea. The library book is soaked. Oh no, oh no, oh no. "Napkins!" I say to no one in particular. Then I run to the lunch line and grab a huge stack. Back at my table I dab the soggy pages.

Please, oh please, let the napkins sop up the juice. The thought of a ruined library book is the absolute worst. I keep pressing the napkins into the damp pages. Then I blow on the pages and waft the book around, hoping to air out the moisture.

"Oh, come on," I whisper. "Dry."

An eighth grader sitting at the table next to mine raises his thick brown eyebrows. I don't know his name. He stares at me.

"Sorry," I mumble.

I set the book down. Talk about embarrassing. Then I blow on the book again, but I do it softly, trying not to draw attention.

After I finish cleaning up my library book, I wipe off the rest of my lunch. Aside from the spilled juice box, the lunch looks good.

I look up as Ridgley places his tray on the table. In the middle of the tray, the beef brisket sticks up like a volcano covered in brown lava. Ridgley takes the seat next to me and pulls *The Cherry Orchard* from his backpack. He doesn't say hello. Instead he begins to read. Which, in my opinion, is the best thing ever.

Ridgley is just beginning *The Cherry Orchard*, and

when he finishes, it'll be the third Chekhov play he's read this week. I'm the one who suggested it.

Ridgley comes to me for play suggestions because he wants to be an actor. I'm happy to help because I love the reading side of Ridgley. The actor side of him I don't really get, but the reading side connects us, always.

I dunk my pita back into the hummus. At the same time, Ridgley pops his nose out from his book and eyes my lunch. I slide the Mediterranean Medley between us. "Want some?"

Ridgley takes a cheese square from the medley. "Thanks." Before he goes back to his play, he asks, "Hey, how's your mom?"

"She got some part in a play."

"That's awesome."

"It's based on a book or something."

"We should see it."

"She's playing the part of a homeless person."

He breathes deeply. "What a range she has."

"The part of a homeless person?"

"I found some old reruns of *The Rich and the Radiant*. Her character, Sloane . . ." Ridgley holds his hand to his chest.

"She was on that show a long time ago."

"Her performance was amazing, and wow oh wow, she had great chemistry with Sebastian."

"Sebastian?"

"Her mysterious brother who appeared in episode three and disappeared by episode four."

"Huh. I had forgotten about Sebastian."

Ridgley leans closer. "Tell me more."

I shrug. "I don't know. I haven't watched my mom's soap in years. I was a little kid when she first got the part. I remember being on set sometimes. She had her own dressing room with her name on the door."

"Wow," he says. Ridgley holds my gaze. "What else?"

Another thought pops into my mind, but there's no way I'm going to tell him. *That's when my parents started fighting, when Mom came home from her show each night.* I shift in my seat, unable to shake off the memory. *She'd always be mad at my dad. Then, after the show was canceled, and they were both in the apartment all the time, the fighting got even worse.*

"We should totally see her play," Ridgley says.

I shrug again. I really like the idea of doing something outside school with Ridgley. We've never done that before. But I wish the thing we were doing was something other than going to my mom's play. I want to ask him to come over to my house, but I feel too nervous to say that out loud.

Ridgley returns to *The Cherry Orchard*. As he reads the play, he whispers the words out loud. *"My father was a peasant, true, but here I am in a white vest and brown shoes . . . like a pearl in an oyster shell."*

I return to my soggy copy of *The Old Man and the Sea* and dab the cover with a napkin. As I dab the book, Ridgley looks up from *The Cherry Orchard*. "Want to go to the play this weekend?"

My heart flutters at the idea of spending time with Ridgley, but then I wonder: Does he want to hang out with me or see my mom perform?

"We can go together," he adds.

I shake my head. "She's still in rehearsals. Show hasn't started."

Ridgley sighs. "Rehearsals." Then he looks right at me. "I really want to be an actor."

"I think you'd be a great actor," I say. I want to add *because I think you're a great person*, but that would be way too embarrassing.

So I return to my book, Ridgley returns to his play, and we spend the last few moments of lunch reading.

chapter four

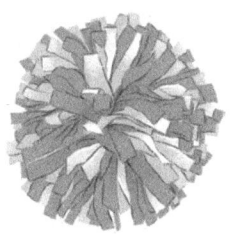

AFTER LUNCH RIDGLEY WALKS NEXT TO ME. We step into the hall, and he looks at the floor. It's odd. Usually while we walk, we talk. It's when we do our talking because we aren't reading. But today Ridgley keeps quiet. He scuffs his motorcycle boots on the floor. They squeak against the shiny linoleum.

Ridgley wears the boots because he thinks they make him look tough, and he thinks actors are supposed to look tough. I disagree. I think actors—I mean *thespians*—should look frail and weak and vulnerable because *thespians* who win Academy Awards play sad, messed-up people. But what do I know about acting, aside from the fact that I never want to do it?

"Sorry about this morning," Ridgley says.

"For what?" I ask.

"You know, in Mr. Perkins's class."

My face grows warm, and my armpits grow warm, and my heart moves toward my throat as I think about how embarrassing that was.

"He called you out, Margaret. That wasn't cool."

I wipe my brow with the back of my hand and readjust my glasses. Ridgley is the only person who calls me Margaret. When we first met, he asked, *Is "Bag" a nickname?* I said, *Yeah.* He asked, *Do you like having a nickname?* I said, *Not really.* He asked, *What's your real name?* I said, *Margaret.* He said, *Can I call you that?* I said, *Yes.* He's called me Margaret ever since.

I usually love when Ridgley says my real name, except now I'm feeling weird. I don't want to talk about this morning. So all I say is "Thanks," because it was nice of Ridgley to understand how embarrassed I was.

"What are you doing after school?" he asks.

"Newport library," I tell him.

"Cool. Want to meet there?"

Ridgley wants to hang out with me after school. I can't think of anything better!

"Sure," I say, trying not to sound too excited.

"Awesome," he says, sounding the same way.

Ridgley sticks his hand into the pocket of his jeans. He wears a white T-shirt, and I'm certain he's got his motorcycle jacket in his locker. In some ways he's like me. He wants his outside to match his inside. Only,

Ridgley's inside is way more interesting than just being tough. On the inside Ridgley is a thinker.

> **Random Thought 730.92**
> Aside from being a reader, being a thinker is the best quality a person can have.

We stop in front of my classroom, room nine, the regular math room. Ridgley pauses. He has class in room ten, the advanced math room. Ridgley is advanced in every subject. Me? I'm only advanced in English, and after this morning's poetry brain fart, I'm feeling as far from advanced as a person can get. The first bell rings above us, as loud as a fire alarm. "See you," I say.

"Bye, Margaret."

Ridgley shuffles across the hall, and I realize I forgot. I'm not going to the Newport library! I don't have a ride.

I turn to tell him I'm staying at school, maybe he wants to stay with me, but the second bell blasts above me before I'm able to get the words out. Ugh. I don't have time. I've got to go to regular math, and, of course, I can't be late for regular math. That's because I have Mrs. Buttocks.

> **Random Thought 574.4**
> Yes, her actual last name is Buttocks,

and yes, it's unbelievable that she's a middle school math teacher and hasn't changed it.

I run into the regular math room because Mrs. Buttocks does not tolerate tardiness. I find my seat without a second to spare.

"Let us begin," she says in a dull voice. "Today we'll be discussing proportions."

"Portions?" I whisper to myself.

"Proportions," she responds.

Not surprisingly, math is awful. I don't understand the lesson at all. What does proportion have to do with numbers anyway? It sounds like something meant for art and design. In my opinion her lesson is completely not math related. Mrs. Buttocks keeps talking about things that don't sound like math, and since I'm not learning anything anyway, I take out *The Old Man and the Sea*, place it on my knees, under my desk, and begin to read.

"What do you think you're doing?"

At first I think it's a question she asks herself. Maybe she doesn't understand what she's teaching? So I keep reading.

"Bag."

I glance away from my book. "Huh?"

She points at my desk. "Hold it up."

I raise *The Old Man and the Sea*, and the class gasps.

"To the principal," Mrs. Buttocks announces.

"It's a classic," I say.

The class bursts into laughter.

"Right now," she says.

It's super unfair, but I know better than to argue with Mrs. Buttocks. She's a lot like a math problem. The answer is right or wrong, and clearly reading a classic work of literature is on the wrong side of her equation.

chapter five

I SPEND THE NEXT HALF HOUR SITTING ON THE bench outside the principal's office, waiting to speak with Principal Doonesbury. When I finally go in, he doesn't ask me to sit.

"What happened?" he wants to know.

"I was reading *The Old Man and the Sea*," I say.

He shakes his head. "Don't let it happen again."

That's it.

If he were a good principal, he'd say, The Old Man and the Sea *is a classic. Good for you, Bag. I know you're hopeless at math, so it's smart of you to use class time to improve your literacy. Carry on with the reading!*

But Principal Doonesbury isn't interested in being a good principal. He's only interested in using as few words as possible to complete his job.

Don't let it happen again.

Unbelievable.

The bell rings, and I trudge out of his office and head to the last class of the day. Life skills. I'm so annoyed about what happened in math that I can barely concentrate. The life skills lesson is about communicating with "I" messages. We sit in a circle. Everyone is encouraged to share. Emily C. goes first.

"I feel embarrassed when Ben rolls his eyes at me."

"You called my layups touchdowns."

"I was cheering for you."

"Touchdowns are football. Not basketball."

"Isn't it all the same?"

"Now, now," Miss Gilder-Lily says. "Let's remember to use the words 'I feel.' Would anyone else like to try?"

I don't raise my hand. I know better than to say how I feel. Because right now I feel extremely annoyed with these "I" messages.

Miss Gilder-Lily sighs. "Do I have a volunteer?"

No one raises a hand. So she sits down at her desk and opens her grade book. "Need I remind you that a large part of your grade is based on class participation?"

A few hands go up in the air. I raise my hand, but only a little, because I don't want a bad grade, but I also don't want to get called on. Lucky for me, the hands around me are raised higher than mine. I don't get called. The "I" messages continue.

"I felt sad when you laughed at my dog. Hooch is a great dog."

"I felt mad that you didn't share your lunch. You had two sandwiches."

"I felt embarrassed when you made fun of my ripped jeans. That's the style. That's the way they're supposed to be!"

I stop listening until I hear the bell ring. Finally. The school day is over. I jump out of my seat and rush out of Miss Gilder-Lily's room.

In the hallway, kids scatter around me like houseflies. Mimi buzzes to cheerleading. Sheldon— I think his name is Sheldon. Shawn, maybe. Shermie? He flies his long legs to basketball. Two eighth graders in black clothing hold hands and breeze out the front entrance together. I trudge down the hall with an urge to swat them all away.

I rush to the water fountain near the cafeteria. Normally I'd meet my mom outside and she'd take me to the library. But of course she's not picking me up. I was hoping I could catch Ridgley as he was leaving school to tell him I won't actually be at the library, but his motorcycle boots are nowhere to be found. And I can't text him or call him, because I don't have a phone.

I knock my foot against the aluminum base, and the water fountain hums back. The hallway chatters with words and laughter. A lonely feeling creeps into my brain, down my neck, and lands in the middle of me. It sits there, heavy and thick. So I wiggle a little, but I can't shake the lonely feeling away.

Come on, Bag, snap out of it. I've got a soggy copy of *The Old Man and the Sea* and an entire afternoon to read it. All I need is a place to sink into my book and forget about the bad things that happened today.

With a sigh I take a seat on the floor next to the fountain. Then I open my backpack and grab *The Old Man and the Sea*. I've read the last page and almost the entire first chapter when I hear Mrs. Buttocks's voice booming from across the hall.

"No loitering!"

"Um," I say.

"Bag." She stops in front of me and looks down. "Reading during my math lesson. And now, reading in the middle of the hallway."

I'm not in the middle of the hallway, I want to say. But I keep the words to myself because I don't want to get in trouble. Even though, technically speaking, I'm right. I'm not in the middle of the hallway. I'm sitting off to the side.

She narrows her eyes as if she knows what I'm not telling her. Then she says, "Tonight's homework is to complete page eighty-four in your math workbook."

I stand up.

"Is anyone coming to get you?" Mrs. Buttocks keeps talking at me. She doesn't talk to me. She talks at me.

"Students are not allowed to wait in the hallway." She looks at my backpack, which is open and filled with homework. "Where is your mother? I can call her for you."

The last thing I need is Mrs. Buttocks calling my mom, telling her she needs to leave rehearsal. Mom will flip, so I say the first thing that comes to my mind. Before I can stop myself, I tell Mrs. Buttocks, "Actually I'm joining cheerleading. I'm just waiting for practice to begin."

"Wonderful," she says. "I had no idea you could dance."

"It runs in my family," I say.

She raises an eyebrow like she doesn't believe me.

I turn away from her. "Better get going." I pick up my backpack, place my book inside, and plan to find a different, more private, spot to read in.

"Not so fast." Mrs. Buttocks checks her watch to see what time it is. It's like the lady has a knack for smelling a lie. "We can go to practice together," she says.

I sigh. There's no way I can wiggle out of this one. So I sling my backpack over my shoulder and head to the gym. Mrs. Buttocks follows me the whole way there.

chapter six

CHEERLEADING BEGINS WITH A WHISTLE. I hear the whistle and then a clap from the other side of a closed door. The door is at the far end of the gym. I've never noticed it before. I have no idea what's inside. Mrs. Buttocks knocks her knuckles against the door. *Tap, tap, tap.* Her knocks are firm and evenly spaced apart. *Tap, tap, tap.* The sound of her knocking syncs up nicely with the whistling and the clapping.

Minerva is going to kill me.

A second later the door opens and a face pops out. It's a woman, about the same age as Mrs. Buttocks. She wears pink lipstick, and when she opens her mouth, I notice a little lipstick smudged on an upper tooth.

The woman smiles and says, "Hello, Buffy!"

Buffy? That's Mrs. Buttocks's first name?

Mrs. Buttocks presses her lips together like she didn't want the woman to say her first name in front of me.

"Hello, Mrs. Yoh," Mrs. Buttocks says in a serious voice.

Mrs. Yoh hops up and down with excitement. Either that or she really needs to pee. "Is there something I can do for you?"

Mrs. Buttocks clears her throat. "My student Bag seems to think she's joining the squad."

"Bag?" Mrs. Yoh pauses like she didn't know I was joining the squad, because I'm not, and I don't want to.

Mrs. Buttocks narrows her eyes at me.

So I think quick and say, "Minerva is my sister."

"Minerva." Mrs. Yoh places a hand on her chest. "What a talent."

"Couldn't agree more," Mrs. Buttocks chimes in. "About Minerva."

Of course Mrs. Buttocks thinks Minerva is talented. In addition to being the cheerleading captain, my sister is the math genius of Thompson Middle School.

Mrs. Yoh looks at me. "Oh dear. Are you here to cheer?"

I freeze solid in place. There is no way I want to cheer.

"We had tryouts earlier in the school year," she says. "Oh my, I'm afraid you missed them."

Thank god, I want to say. But then I remember, Mrs. Buttocks is standing right next to me. I ask Mrs. Yoh, "Can I stay and watch?"

Mrs. Yoh claps her hands together. "What a wonderful idea! Minerva will be thrilled to see you!"

No, she won't, I want to say. But I keep the words to myself. Obviously Mrs. Yoh and Mrs. Buttocks love Minerva. They don't want to hear anything other than how wonderful she is. There is also the unfortunate fact that I've got nowhere else to go. There's no way I want to wait for my mom with Mrs. Buttocks.

Mrs. Buttocks taps my arm, reminding me, "Homework is to complete page eighty-four."

Then Mrs. Buttocks leaves, and Mrs. Yoh shoos me through the door. Not a moment later I find myself in a room filled with cheerleaders. The room is tiny and bright and crowded. And when I say "room," I don't mean an actual room. The space is more like a closet. In fact, that's exactly what this is, an old storage closet. Along with glass cleaner, brooms, mops, and paper towels, the cheerleaders have filled it with their beauty products.

I sigh, and smell hair spray and nail polish remover and strawberry lip gloss. The room makes me want to run to the Newport Bridge, breathe out the scent of chemicals, and breathe in the scent of the ocean. The cheerleaders are talking and talking and talking and putting on makeup. Minerva is nowhere in sight.

Mrs. Yoh grabs my upper arm and squeezes it. "I love that your name is 'Bag.'"

"It's a nickname," I mumble.

"It's marvelous!" She keeps squeezing my arm.

I don't like being touched, and I really want her to take her hand away from me. I look down at my T-shirt. I DON'T PLAY SPORTS. It's the exact wrong thing to wear in a room filled with cheerleaders wearing matching uniforms.

"Where's my sister?" I ask.

"Let's get going, girls!" Mrs. Yoh gives me another squeeze.

Please, oh please, don't let her squeeze me anymore.

"Now, girls." Mrs. Yoh claps her hands together. "I'd like to introduce you to Bag, Minerva's little sister!"

"We know Bag," Mimi says in a dull voice. I wonder if she's still mad that I interrupted her in English.

Just as my name is said, Minerva enters the storage closet. Everyone turns to look at her.

Mrs. Yoh says, "Minerva, there you are. Now chop-chop, dear. Get your hair into a ponytail. We're about to start practice."

Minerva glares at me.

"I didn't plan on coming," I explain quickly. "I was reading in the hallway, and then Mrs. Buttocks . . ."

I stop talking under the intensity of my sister's withering glare.

Minerva looks up at the ceiling. "Please tell me this is not happening."

Mrs. Yoh gasps. "Oh! I have the most wonderful

idea!" She motions toward a pile of tangled pom-poms. "Bag, would you like to help us today?"

"Help you?" She can't be serious.

She continues, "We could use a hand with these pom-poms. We also need to slide some of the bleachers over, and oh, there's the foam mats that need to be dragged out from the closet."

"Um," I say.

"It would be a huge help," she adds.

I don't want to stay with the cheerleaders. But more than that, I don't want to leave the gym and bump into Mrs. Buttocks again. At this point she'd probably have me suspended.

I look at my sister. Her face has grown pale, and her jaw tightens. Her lips pinch together. I get that she doesn't want me here, but her reaction seems a bit dramatic. My sister seriously looks unwell.

"Absolutely do not stay," she says to me.

"Now, Minerva," Mrs. Yoh says. "We could use the help."

Minerva keeps staring at me, waiting for me to leave. Then Minerva leans toward Mimi. She whispers something into Mimi's ear. They both start to laugh. Minerva looks back at me, laughing.

I want to leave, but I can't leave. I stare at Minerva's perfect hair, her perfect uniform, and the little burn hole at the bottom. What's going on with her?

Mrs. Yoh puts her arm around me. "What do you say? Can you give us a hand?"

Even though Mrs. Yoh is speaking to me, I'm thinking about my sister. I want to know what she was whispering to Mimi. I want to know how she got that burn hole. I want to know why she wasn't at practice when I first got here. I want to know if something is seriously wrong with her.

All signs point to yes.

"How about it, Bag?" Mrs. Yoh waits for me to respond. "Can you stay?"

I study my sister. She's glaring at me again, a total death stare. I don't look away, and she doesn't either. It feels like we're in a standoff.

I turn to Mrs. Yoh. "Yes," I say. "Count me in."

"Wonderful!" she replies.

I may not know what Minerva is hiding, but I do know that she's hiding something. And I'm in the exact right place to find out what it is.

chapter seven

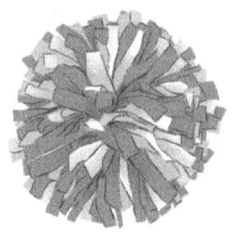

FIFTY-NINE MISERABLE MINUTES LATER I'M still untangling pom-poms. I sit in a sea of blue-and-orange plastic ribbons. The more I try to pull the tangles apart, the bigger the tangles become. My hand cramps in the area between my thumb and pointer finger.

I look up at the ceiling of the storage closet. There is a brown stain directly above where I'm sitting. I look back down at the pom-poms. It really would be so much better if I was reading at the Newport Public Library. Which reminds me of Ridgley. If he went to the library, I hope he didn't look for me. Ugh. The pom-poms stay spread across my lap as the cheerleaders practice a cheer in the gym called "Shake It, Shake It, Shake It till You Make It."

"Work that booty, move those hips, dribble that ball, and..."

The girls hold their hands up to the ceiling.

"We'll flip!" they shout.

I watch them from the storage closet. The door is wide open. I wait for someone to flip. Nobody flips. The cheerleaders stay on their feet. The cheer ends. Which seems like false advertising to me.

Random Thought 792.8

If you say you're going to flip, I think
you should flip.

"Now, now," Mrs. Yoh announces. "Excellent work, everyone. Time to pack up, and let's not forget, we've got a new cheer to learn tomorrow. So get a good night's sleep tonight. And let's thank Bag for her help with the equipment!"

No one says thank you.

I drop the pom-poms into a messy pile and head for the door.

"Bag?" Mrs. Yoh calls into the storage closet. "Please put the pom-poms in the bin."

I sigh. "Okay, Mrs. Yoh." There's a plastic bin in the corner of the storage closet. I grab the pom-poms, shuffle to the corner of the room, and shove the tangled mess inside. The cheerleaders let out a final squeal. Then they rush out of the gym together as I slam the top of the bin down. After that, I leave the storage closet, leave the gym, and head outside, wishing I were in the library.

Outside Minerva sits with Emily S., Emily C., and Mimi.

"Too cute."

"Totally."

"Love that."

"So much."

I have no idea what they're actually talking about.

I take a seat on a bench near the parking lot. I'm wearing my T-shirt, and on top of that a hoodie, and on top of that my bright red Salvation Army coat. Even with all my layers, I can't stop shivering.

One by one the girls get picked up by moms and nannies and older siblings and dads. We watch everyone leave as the area in front of the gym grows empty, with the exception of Minerva, Mrs. Yoh, and me.

The sky is black and starless. The air is bitterly cold. My breath blows in long snakelike strips of white. My nose is numb, my cheeks are numb, and my eyes hurt when I squint. It's as if I can picture the freezing air blowing off the ocean, swirling up Spring Street, and landing directly in my face.

Spring Street. That's where the Newport Public Library is located. I picture Ridgley reading another

Chekhov play in a squishy chair near a library window. . . . I really wish I was reading next to him right now. I hope he isn't upset because I didn't show up.

Mrs. Yoh stays with us in front of the school. I can tell she's cold, but she tries to keep cheery. She smiles a big, toothy grin and says, "Oh my word! It sure is nippy out here!"

Minerva and I don't say anything.

Finally Mrs. Yoh asks, "Can I drive you girls home?"

I look at the ground. It's so embarrassing. Mom didn't pick us up. I wonder if she forgot. I wonder if she's still at rehearsal.

"Girls?" Mrs. Yoh says. "Do you need a ride?"

"Our mom's on her way," Minerva says in a quiet voice.

"Can you call her?" Mrs. Yoh asks.

Minerva slumps into her puffy coat and wraps her arms around herself.

I stare at Mrs. Yoh and say, "We don't have phones." I leave out the part that we can't afford them. Mom has a cell for her business and that's it. One phone. Three family members. It's a huge bummer.

"I know!" Mrs. Yoh stands up and claps her hands together. It's unbelievable how this woman can stay chipper. "Why don't I pull my car around, and we can sit inside and warm up until your mom comes?"

Even though I've shared a lot of space with Mrs. Yoh

this afternoon, I can't wait to sit in her car. I've never felt so cold. Seriously, my body is like a pint of vanilla ice cream covered in freezer burn. I usually love night air, but this is downright miserable.

Mrs. Yoh walks down the circle driveway toward the faculty lot to get her car. Minerva sighs. "So annoying."

"She's just being nice," I say.

"No. I mean Mom."

"Oh yeah. That."

"Where is she?" Minerva asks.

"Maybe rehearsal ran late?"

We both grow quiet, and even though Minerva has bothered me to no end today, I'm glad she's here. Waiting alone would be way worse.

Random Thought 160
When you love someone, it's not because of lovely things. Love has nothing to do with nice feelings and hearts and stars and magic. I think love is the opposite. When people love one another, it's because they understand what is hurting.

chapter eight

WE SIT IN MRS. YOH'S CAR FOR A LONG TIME. Long enough for me to know that Mrs. Yoh's car has a mustard-yellow dashboard, itchy brown upholstery, and an ashtray filled with coins.

Mrs. Yoh sits in the driver's seat with the car running. She keeps fidgeting with her hands like she's uncomfortable with the silence.

"So," she says, breaking the quiet, "what brought you girls to Rhode Island?"

I'm not sure how to respond. Do I mention that our parents were fighting a lot in New York, Mom ran out of money, and then right after we got here, Dad moved out of the house?

Minerva doesn't respond either.

Mrs. Yoh continues, "I understand you moved from

Manhattan. Do you have family in the area? That must have been quite an adjustment. Moving from the big city!"

I nod. "It was."

"So, what brought you here?" she asks again.

I shrug. "My mom likes the license plate."

Mrs. Yoh laughs like she doesn't believe me.

"The Rhode Island plate has a wave," I explain.

Minerva glares at me.

"What?" I raise my eyebrows at her. "That's what Mom says. Rhode Island has the best license plate."

Minerva rolls her eyes and then turns to Mrs. Yoh. "I'm glad we moved, Mrs. Yoh. I like it here. I especially like cheerleading."

"Oh, that's so nice to hear," Mrs. Yoh replies.

Everyone goes back to being quiet. It feels awkward, the quiet. We sit there for what feels like hours, until Mom's truck finally pulls into the school's circular driveway. Minerva jumps out of Mrs. Yoh's car faster than a cat fleeing from a pack of dogs. I hang back with Mrs. Yoh.

"Thanks," I say, "for waiting with us."

"My pleasure."

Then I scoot out of Mrs. Yoh's car. She rolls down the passenger-side window and leans her head toward it. "Practice those steps, Minerva! And, Bag, I'd love to see you again tomorrow!"

I rush to Mom's truck, and the cold wind slams against my body. Before I get in, Mom says frantically, "I had to get the Tupperware bins from Wheeler Elementary because the school couldn't find them, and when I got there, they were missing lids. I mean, who doesn't keep the lids with Tupperware?"

Minerva scoots over to the middle seat. I take the spot next to the window. Then I slam the door shut and rub my hands together. Minerva doesn't say anything.

"Have you been waiting long?" Mom asks.

"Yes," I say, because it's the truth.

"I'm sorry," she says.

"It's okay," I say, because I don't want Mom to keep apologizing.

"No, it isn't," Minerva cuts in.

"Minerva." Mom pulls the truck out of the driveway. "I get that you're mad, but—"

"I'm not mad," my sister screams. "I'm furious!"

"It wasn't my—"

"What, Mom? Your fault? Of course it's your fault! First you stick me with Bag. Then you stick me in Mrs. Yoh's car *with* Bag. Ugh!" Minerva covers her face with her hands. "This has been the worst day of my life."

"Gee, thanks," I say.

"You'd better not be at practice tomorrow," she replies.

We drive the rest of the way home without any

words. I lean my head against the window. My window. Finally I've gotten away from the middle seat.

But I realize that my moment away from the middle seat doesn't even matter. Normally I'd love nothing more than to sit next to the window and roll it down. But there's too much bad stuff going on to enjoy it. For starters I'm cold. Another thing, Minerva hurt my feelings.

Random Thought 118
When you've had an awful day, the
window seat doesn't feel like the window
seat. When you've had an awful day,
every seat feels like the middle.

Back at home we move around the house separately. Not because we're still fighting but because that's what we do when we're home. We stay in our own spaces.

In the kitchen Mom unpacks Tupperware containers at the sink. In the bathroom Minerva takes a shower as steam trickles out under the bathroom door. As for me, I rush to my room and pull out *The Old Man and the Sea*. It has a purple stain on the back cover from the spilled juice box. I open to page twelve, and the left corner is wrinkled and, like the cover, stained. I feel like the worst person for damaging a library book. But I guess what would be worse is to damage a library book and then not read it. So I get to work.

Page twelve is a picture of the boy and the old man, which is cool because it only takes me a second to read that page. But now page thirteen looms in front of me. Page thirteen has extremely long paragraphs, no dialogue, and no pictures. Also known as not fun. But I like the book so far. It's about bad luck and fishing. The fishing part I don't relate to, but the bad luck part is right up my alley.

But he knew he had attained it and he knew it was not disgraceful . . .

I pull my eyes away from the unfinished sentence. I've got this long page ahead of me, and I can't focus. So I close my eyes. In the dark a question pours into my head. What was Minerva doing at the beginning of practice? Where was she? Why was she late? How come she didn't get in trouble?

I open my eyes and place a bookmark in page thirteen. I always use a bookmark because once a page is doggie-eared, the crease never goes away. The book is scarred forever. I wish more people understood this.

Random Thought 158.1
I wish more people paid attention to the
little things.

My question about Minerva stays stuck in my head. My head is too full for me to read. So I place *The Old Man and the Sea* on my bedside table and go look for her.

She's in the living room, on the couch, and her hair is wrapped in a white towel. She's got a stack of homework in her lap. Also, in pure Minerva fashion, she's watching *The Bachelor.*

On the screen two women yell at each other. One woman has a pixie cut, and the other has long curly hair. The pixie-cut woman throws a drink onto the curly-haired woman, and then the curly-haired woman starts to cry.

"Is it a competition for being tough or pretty?" I ask.

"Pretty. No one cares how tough they are."

Now both women are crying.

"You like watching this?" I ask. "I mean, what do these people do in their spare time? Read? Write? Play the ukulele?" Minerva's eyes stay locked on the screen. So I peer over her shoulder. "Isn't it hard to do math with the TV on?"

"Go away."

"Why weren't you at practice today? You know, at the beginning?"

"Not your business," she says.

"Don't you like cheerleading?" I ask.

"I'm in charge of writing the cheers. That's where I was." She flips the papers over and glares at me. "Would you leave already?"

"Sheesh," I say. "It was only a question."

"Eat rat poison and die."

"Nice, Minerva."

I'm about to ask her about the burn hole, when Mom shouts my name. "Baggie! Can you come here? I need your help."

I shake my head at my sister. It's probably better that Mom interrupted us. If Minerva got mad at me for asking about practice, imagine how mad she'd be if I asked her about the hole in her skirt. Even worse, maybe she doesn't know the hole is there. Maybe I'd be the one to tell her and then she'd really freak out at me.

I leave my sister and find Mom in her room. She's sitting on her bed reading a stack of papers. Her hair is pulled back in a messy bun. Mom looks up from her script and smiles. "What do you think of this line?" She clears her throat and gets into character. *"You can't live in fear of something as basic as fire."*

Mom stops acting and looks at me. "Do you think the character's being sarcastic? I'm reading it as though she's giving advice, but maybe it's more layered than that?" Mom picks up the paper again. "But what if it's sarcasm?" Mom twirls her hair and stares at the manuscript. "What do you think?"

I shrug. "I don't know, Mom. It's just one sentence."

"Oh, it's more than one sentence. These words are very important to the story. They're establishing a pivotal moment in this woman's life, how she's a woman, how she's a mother, how she sees the world. . . ."

"Hang on!" she says. Mom hands me the manuscript. "How about you read a few lines? I'd love to hear how the play sounds coming from someone else!"

Me? Read out loud? Doesn't she know me at all?

"No thanks," I say.

"Please, Baggie." Mom points to the middle of the page. "Start here. Right below the fire line."

I clear my throat so I don't feel as embarrassed about reading out loud. I decide I'll take one word at a time and go nice and slow. I'd rather read slow and get it right than read fast and mess up the words.

"Don't worry," I say. *"God understands. He knows that your father is a cross we must bear."*

"That's it!" Mom exclaims. "She's vulnerable. She's broken and vulnerable, and she's being one hundred percent honest with her children. That's where her words are coming from."

I stare at the manuscript. "All from this one line?"

"Thanks so much for reading, sweetheart. You did an excellent job." Mom kisses the top of my head and takes the paper from my hands.

I feel great about reading out loud and not messing up. Mom goes back to her script. I go back to my room.

But the words from her play stay in my head. *Your*

father is a cross we must bear. I wonder if Mom, not the actress mom but my real mom, feels that way about Dad, not the dad from the play but my real dad. I hope not. He moved out of our house shortly after we moved here. She's the one who asked him to leave. I don't know why. I mean, they fought a lot, but don't all parents fight a lot? Now Mom never wants to talk about him. Neither does Minerva. But Mom still has one of his sweaters, tucked in the back of her closet, which must mean she misses him. I know I sure do.

Sometimes Mom lets me call him from her phone. When we talk, I ask, *When are you coming back?* He says, *We'll see.* I say, *I miss you.* He says, *I miss you too, Maggie.* I say, *Mom has one of your sweaters tucked in the back of her closet.* He says, *Huh.* We say, *Goodbye.* I say, *I love you.* He always says, *I love you too.*

When I try to talk to Mom about him, when I ask her when he's coming home, she presses her lips together like she doesn't want to talk about it. Then she says, *We'll see.* Which is a terrible answer because, if you ask me, "We'll see" is just a nice way of saying "I have no idea."

I don't want to think about this anymore, so I grab my backpack and get back to work. Mrs. Buttocks doesn't accept late homework. She also doesn't accept excuses.

After I finish my math homework, I open *The Old Man and the Sea*, page thirteen. But when I try to read the words, I can't concentrate. There's a buzzing coming from my lightbulb, my math homework didn't make any sense, and I still don't know what's going on with my sister.

I set the book on my bedside table. Then I take off my glasses and rub the bridge of my nose. I love doing this because it makes me feel like a bookworm. Not a moment later Mom peeks her head into my room. "Hello in here."

She's got green gunk all over her face. I bolt up and make a face.

"What?" she says.

"Your skin," I say.

Mom laughs. "Oh, this." She sticks her finger into the green stuff. "Sorry, I forgot I had it on. It's just a little mask. For my wrinkles."

"You put that on your skin on purpose?"

"Ha," she says. "I always forget you're the comedian of the family."

"I thought you were playing a homeless person."

"I am."

"Then don't you want wrinkles? You know, to look more homeless?"

Mom looks up and shakes her hair away from her face. "All actresses must maintain an element of beauty." She pouts her lips the same way her character Sloane did on *The Rich and the Radiant*. "After all," she continues, "one role leads to the next, and I don't want to limit my options."

Then Mom moves toward me, pulls up my blanket, and tucks the top part under my chin. "Cozy, cozy." I make a face and pretend I don't like being tucked in, but the truth is, I love it. I love the weight of the blanket. I love how it snuggles under my chin and wraps around the sides of my body. I love that my mom does it just right.

"'Night, Mom."

"Good night," she says.

Then she closes my door softly, and then my room is quiet, aside from the humming that comes from the lightbulb. I turn off the lamp next to my bed. The room is dark and quiet. My mind starts to race. I think about reading *The Old Man and the Sea* and Mrs. Buttocks and the tangled pom-poms and Mrs. Yoh and cheerleading practice and Minerva.

Minerva.

Why was she late for practice? Was she really writing cheers? Where was she writing them? How come she didn't come into the storage closet with a new cheer in hand? My head swirls full of questions. I don't have answers for any of them.

Minerva.

She's hiding something. I know it. She might not want me at cheerleading practice, but there's no way I'm backing down now. I fall asleep with a book beside my bed and a plan inside my head. I'm going to get to the bottom of this. Tomorrow I'm going to find out what my sister is hiding.

chapter nine

THE NEXT MORNING, ON THE WAY TO SCHOOL, I'm back in the middle seat. At least Minerva doesn't switch on the heat.

Even better, Mom drives slowly and barely elbows me as she turns onto Spring. She's got her Lunches by Lenore loaded in the truck and her homeless costume tucked in her purse.

I gaze out the windshield. The sky is filled with clouds the color of the rocks at Purgatory Cove. I love the weather, cool and still and uncomplicated. Plus, Minerva is giving me the silent treatment. It's a double dose of awesome, the gloomy weather and a quiet Minerva.

Minerva's not wearing her uniform because it's not School Spirit Day. Instead she's got on a blue-and-white striped sweater under a white puffer coat. Her hair is in a perfect ponytail. Mom pulls up in front of school and hits the brake pedal. The squeak is so loud, I worry the brakes might not work anymore. Thankfully, the truck comes to a stop.

The moment it does, Minerva zips her coat and swings the door open. Her feet hit the icy pavement, and she tosses her backpack over her shoulder. The backpack looks like it has a week's worth of homework. Which is strange, a week's worth of homework for one night.

Minerva wraps her arms around herself and groans. "It'd better not snow." Then, without saying goodbye, she rushes toward school.

I turn to Mom, and before I get out of the truck, I say, "So, I'll stay at school and you can pick me up with Minerva."

Mom's face relaxes like she's relieved I'm not complaining about the library. "Should I meet you here or at the gym?" she asks.

"The gym," I say quickly.

I scoot out from the middle seat. Before I head for school, I look back at her. Mom checks her phone, and the lines on her forehead go deeper. By the look of her forehead, I'd say that mask she's been using is having the opposite effect on her wrinkles. I don't want her forehead to be so wrinkly. I don't want her to feel so stressed.

So I shout, "Thanks for the ride, Mom!"

She pulls away from the curb, and I wonder if she even heard me.

I scuff my sneaker against the pavement and turn to school. At the same time, Minerva takes a fast left and darts toward the south wall.

It's weird. The south wall is near the cafeteria kitchen, and the south wall is lined with dumpsters. My sister hates smelly things. I've got no idea why she'd purposely go near the grossest area of school.

I watch Minerva's puffy white coat disappear around the corner. She reminds me of a cloud that has the ability to evaporate into thin air.

A bus pulls up behind me, and the brakes squeak and lurch as the oversized wheels roll to a stop. My eyes stay locked on the spot where Minerva just disappeared. School doesn't start for another twenty minutes. Why is my sister headed for the dumpsters? Because I can't think of a single reason, there's only one thing left to do.

I follow her.

chapter ten

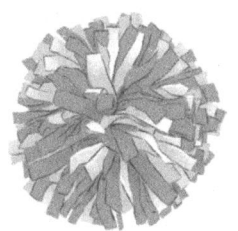

I CREEP AROUND THE CORNER AND KEEP MY back pressed against the wall. The bricks feel like blocks of ice against my body, and the mortar between them snags at my wool coat. I turn up my red collar and cozy it under my chin. Then, with my back still against the wall, I move toward where my sister is hiding. Before I see her, I hear her.

"Wait two minutes," she says. My sister's voice is loud and bossy. "If you go sooner," she adds, "there might be teachers, and if it's later, you won't have enough time. Got it?"

"Yes, Minerva," a voice says back.

Then the voices grow quiet. I inch closer. I take a turn along the south wall and drop down onto my knees, still with my back pressing against the cold bricks.

Minerva.

Minerva is standing next to a dumpster with Mimi Fookwire. Mimi's curly brown hair spills out from a pink hat with a white pom-pom on top.

"Where's the list?" Minerva asks.

"I have it, Minerva." Mimi holds up a piece of paper. "Right here."

"Quiet," Minerva barks. She pulls her head out from behind the dumpster. "You never know who could be listening." Minerva grabs the list out of Mimi's hand. I keep moving closer to see what's on the list when Minerva snaps, "Is someone there?"

Minerva crouches behind the dumpster and pulls Mimi next to her. I can't see Minerva and Mimi, but I can hear them whispering. I can't tell what they're whispering about, except for the word "list." I inch even closer. Then Minerva pops her face out from the metal dumpster.

"Agh!" I stumble back.

Her hazel eyes meet mine. She has the exact same color eyes as Mom. Neither one of us knows what to say. Finally Mimi peeks her little face out from behind the dumpster, and with a tiny voice, she says, "Bag?"

My gaze stays locked on Minerva. My sister whispers one word at a time, which is way scarier than the sound of her shouting. "What. Are. You. Doing. Here."

Inside, my body trembles. Outside, I pretend I'm

strong. I stand up straight, adjust my glasses, and say, "I was about to ask you the same thing."

Minerva folds her list, and I notice that *her* hands are trembling. Is she scared? Cold? Angry? Minerva shivers like a leaf on a rickety branch.

"What list were you talking about?" I ask.

Mimi gasps. "How do you know about the list?"

"Shut your mouth," Minerva says. She shoves the list into the pocket of her puffer coat. She's not trembling anymore, and she looks nothing like a leaf. "The list is no biggie. Just a bunch of cheers Mrs. Yoh asked me to write. Didn't you know? I'm in charge of writing the cheers."

"Yeah, I remember. You've mentioned that before."

"The only thing she put you in charge of was the equipment," Mimi says to me.

Minerva laughs. "Imagine my sister writing cheers," she says.

"They'd all be spelled wrong," Mimi says. "Like in Mr. Perkins's class. She spells things wrong all the time."

My breath catches. It feels like I just got kicked in the gut. Neither one of them knows about my dyslexia, and I'm not about to tell them. They'd make fun of me even more.

Now both Minerva and Mimi are laughing.

My face grows hot, and my hands are freezing. I keep my hands in my pockets. Then I try to make an *L* with my thumb and pointer finger to figure out which hand is my left. I want to know my right from my left because sometimes it's hard to tell, and right now I just want to know something. But when I make the *L*, I can't tell. I don't know which hand is which. Both hands feel like *L*'s.

Minerva brushes past me and slings her backpack over her shoulder. Before she leaves, she turns around and says, "You'd better not be at practice today."

Mimi scoots away from the dumpster and trails my sister like a little dog hoping for a scrap of food. Neither one of them says goodbye to me. Minerva never even turns around to see if I'm still standing next to the dumpsters.

Why would she hide behind the disgusting dumpsters to write cheers? She can write her cheers anywhere. My sister might treat me like an idiot, but deep down in the pit of my stomach, I know.

I know she's lying.

chapter eleven

I WALK THROUGH SCHOOL IN A DAZE. THE HALLWAYS are bustling with people who talk and text, whisper and chew gum. It's like I'm here but not here. I'm watching from some other place as I step one foot in front of the other and catch pieces of conversations.

How to boil an egg.

Sweaty armpits.

Forgotten homework.

Naming a dog.

Lice.

Their words float in and out of my brain. Nobody says anything about Minerva or Mimi or the dumpsters or the list of "cheers" or whatever was actually written on that piece of paper.

The first bell wails above me, and I get myself to

science. When that class ends, I get myself to geography, then life skills, then math. The ordering of classes changes each day, which is pretty confusing. I have to think about where I have to be and when I have to be there. Fortunately, I haven't made any mistakes this year. At least not yet. Lunch is always at the same time.

Today lunch is eventful. I haven't seen Mimi since the dumpsters. Or Minerva. Come to think of it, I haven't seen Ridgley either. Which is very odd. Usually we find each other between classes.

I coast down the hallway, and thoughts slip from my head like a melting Popsicle. I don't know where Ridgley is. I don't know what Minerva is lying about. My thoughts and worries and questions and fears drip out of me. By sixth period my head doesn't feel attached to my body.

It's amazing I make it to English.

"Greetings, Earthlings!"

Mr. Perkins is in a good mood. He's wearing a brown blazer, his scraggly hair is brushed, and he's got a T-shirt under his jacket that says BUCK THE SYSTEM. It's totally a shirt my dad would wear. I love it.

Also, like yesterday, Mr. Perkins's wooden desk has nothing on it—no papers, no books, not even a pencil. The fluorescent lights make the varnished wood sparkle.

Ridgley walks into the room. I worry about yesterday. Did he go to the library?

"Hey," I call out.

"Hey," Ridgley says.

Then the bell blares above us and Mimi steps into the classroom. I wish I had time to talk to Ridgley. I hope he didn't look for me at the library.

"Just made it," Mr. Perkins tells Mimi.

Mimi doesn't look at me. Instead she slips into her assigned seat next to mine. It's like we never even saw each other this morning.

"Today we're sticking with poetry," Mr. Perkins says. "Today I'd like to put pen to paper and see what we come up with."

Oh no. He wants us to write poetry. How am I going to write poetry? I can barely organize the thoughts in my head, let alone write a poem.

"To begin," he says, "let's talk about blank space. Does anyone know what I mean when I say 'blank space'?"

Ridgley doesn't raise his hand. Instead he calls out in a dumb voice, "It's like outer space with no lights on." He laughs like an actor in a play trying too hard to make a bad joke work.

Mr. Perkins shakes his head. "Ridgley, I think we both know that's not what 'blank space' means." He turns to face me. "How about you, Bag? Whatcha got?"

"Uh—" I don't know what to say, and I already made a fool of myself about the Sharon Creech thing, and now I don't know how to describe blank space, and I want to impress Mr. Perkins, and I want to talk about poetry, but I have so many other things floating inside me.

"She doesn't know what it means," Mimi says in a nasty voice, a tiny voice, a voice that sounds like an attack. "Bag doesn't know anything."

"Yes, I do," I snipe back.

Then without thinking I point to Mr. Perkins's desk. "Blank space is kind of like your desk, Mr. Perkins. Usually it's covered with books and papers and your half-drunk cup of coffee." The class giggles, and an idea forms inside my head.

"Go on," Mr. Perkins says.

"Well, now your desk is bare, and that says a lot. It says more than all that stuff you usually have. Which is the same in poetry. When there's blank space on the page, it makes the reader pay attention."

"Wonderful!" Mr. Perkins brings his hands together in one big clap.

I feel great, but then I feel worried because Ridgley never catches my eye to give me a thumbs-up like he usually does when I get an answer right. Maybe he did try to look for me at the library? What if he's upset that I didn't show up? And Mimi's nasty comment still sits with me. *Bag doesn't know anything.*

A bell rings, indicating English has ended.

I jump up from my desk and head straight for Ridgley. Then I stop in front of his desk. He's placing a book into his backpack. It's a Chekhov play called *Uncle Vanya*.

"I'm sorry about yesterday," I say.

Ridgley flings his backpack onto his back, looks at the floor, shoves his hands into his pockets.

"Did you go?" I ask. "To the library?"

"Yeah."

"Oh gosh. I'm so sorry."

"No biggie," he says.

"I mean, I didn't have a ride."

Ridgley finally looks up. I can't tell if he's mad or sad or happy. He has a blank expression.

"Because of my mom's play," I explain. "She couldn't drive me to the library, so I wasn't able to go."

"I thought you changed your mind," he says.

"No way! I totally wanted to go."

"Oh," he says.

"No-brainer," I reply.

"Are you going today?" he asks.

"Can't. My mom has rehearsals again. I'm staying after school with my sister."

Minerva pops into my mind. What was she doing at those dumpsters? Did she go back? Where is Minerva?

"I've got to go," I tell Ridgley. "I'll explain more later!"

chapter twelve

AFTER ANOTHER DIFFICULT SPANISH CLASS, IT'S the end of the day. I rush to the gym and open the door. Hot air whooshes into my face. The gym smells like BO and bubble gum. I shield my nose with my hand, but I can't escape the overwhelming smell.

Sneakers squeak against the gym floor. A bunch of basketball players are running, stopping, turning, sprinting, and smacking their sneakers against the shiny floor. Half the boys wear shirts. The other half do not.

I feel embarrassed standing on the edge of the gym staring at a bunch of half-naked boys. My face grows hot, and my armpits gets sticky. The boys continue to race the length of the gym.

Then a whistle blows and the boys run to the foul line.

"Wind sprints," the coach yells. "Go!"

The word "go" kicks me into gear. I have to find Minerva. So I head toward the storage closet as if I'm running a wind sprint of my own.

Out of breath, I pause in the doorframe of the storage closet. The cheerleaders are there. They've got on stretchy pants, tank tops, white socks, and sneakers. None of them sees me. They're too busy clapping to notice me watching them from the door. They kneel, clap their hands together, and then slap their hands against the floor.

Clap, clap, slap. Clap, clap, slap.

The clapping and slapping sound surprisingly good, so good that I want to join in. But then the cheerleaders start to chant.

"We love, we love, baskets. Yay! Shoot and score! We love, we love, baskets. Yay! Shoot and score!"

I prefer when they do the clapping and slapping, way more than the chanting. I'm so caught up with the cheering that I almost forget why I'm here in the first place. Then my eyes search the room for my sister. I see a pile of pom-poms in the corner, a laptop in another corner, and a hair dryer plugged into the wall. My sister isn't here.

"Bag?"

A high-pitched voice calls out behind me. I freeze in the doorframe, and then I turn around. Mrs. Yoh.

"Oh!" she says. "Bag, I'm so glad to see you! We sure

could use your help with the equipment. I've got these pom-poms to untangle, and we've got to make our list for the game tomorrow." She points to the pile of pom-poms. "There's no time like the present."

I look at the pom-poms and nod. Then I look back at Mrs. Yoh. "Where's my sister?"

"Writing cheers, of course."

"She gets to leave the group by herself?"

"She's with Mimi."

"Do they leave practice a lot?"

"Bag, creating a work of art takes time and focus. Your sister has real vision."

Vision? Minerva watches reruns of *The Bachelor* seven days a week. How much vision could she possibly have?

Mrs. Yoh smiles at me. "Your sister is writing a new cheer as we speak."

"Where does she write the cheers?"

"The cafeteria, of course. Now what do you say, Bag? How about helping us with the equipment?"

"Sure," I say. "I'll be right back!"

"Where are you going?" she asks.

"The bathroom," I lie.

"Alrighty then. Make it quick," she says. "Those pom-poms aren't going to untangle themselves."

I race out of the storage closet and sprint like the wind while this morning's conversation races inside my head.

I remember Minerva talking about two minutes.

I remember Mimi looking scared.

I remember Minerva saying she's writing cheers.

I remember not believing her.

When I get a few feet away from the cafeteria, I stop running. I'm breathing hard. I bend over and collect myself before I get closer. I don't want Minerva to hear me.

Then I creep toward the cafeteria like a cat hiding in a dark alley.

I want to catch Minerva in the act, whatever that act might be. I stay close to the wall and use the pads of my fingertips to silently open the door.

Inside, the cafeteria floor shines. The tables are freshly wiped and wet with water. The trash bins are empty. The lunch trays are neatly stacked on the table next to the trash. The room smells like glass cleaner. Sunlight trickles through tall windows.

Random Thought 259

I've never been to church, but I imagine
this is what it feels like. Not that church
is a cafeteria, but this good feeling that
everything is in place and smells nice,
and sunlight is able to dance on the
tables.

The room is so beautiful, I almost forget why I'm here. That's when I realize, Minerva. Minerva is not in the cafeteria.

Where is she? Where is Mimi? Mrs. Yoh said they were writing cheers in the cafeteria. Think. Where would they be? The bathroom? I turn to go, and the moment I do, the exit door creaks open.

I freeze. The exit door is in the far right corner of the cafeteria. Outside the exit door the wall is lined with dumpsters. The same dumpsters Minerva and Mimi were hiding behind this morning.

Without a sound I drop to the floor. I'm on hands and knees, crouched under a lunch table. I can't see who walks through the door, but I hear footsteps. The footsteps land as soft as cotton balls on the linoleum floor. I stay still. The footsteps come closer, and I see a pair of tiny white sneakers. They're a table length away from me. The shoes do not belong to my sister. I tilt my head and see stretchy black pants, a small hand, and—wait a minute.

A burn mark.

A burn mark?

I see a red burn mark on her thumb. I also see black smudges from ash on the tip of her index finger. I remember the burn hole in my sister's skirt. *Is* it Minerva? I shake my head. No. The hands are too small. The sneakers are too small. The footsteps are too quiet. I squint my eyes at the fingers. As the person passes me, then walks away from me, I can see more of her. My eyes scan farther up, and I see a gray sweatshirt, a gold heart necklace, and finally I see Mimi Fookwire.

Her tiny face frowns as she heads for the cafeteria door. She has no idea I'm hiding under a lunch table.

She pushes the door open.

She is gone.

The door swings open and shut and open and shut.

At the same time, my head does its own opening and shutting. I have no idea why her hand is burned. I have no idea where my sister is. I have no idea what in the world is behind those dumpsters.

So I do the only logical thing.

I go to the dumpsters.

Outside, next to the exit door, three green dumpsters line the brick wall. The dark green metal is rusted in places and bent in others.

"Minerva?" I whisper.

The smell of rotten meatloaf floods my nose, and it's the worst ever, erasing the good smell of glass cleaner in the cafeteria.

I want to go back inside, but I see a small pile of ashes. I kneel and lean down until my face is inches away from the pile. It is small, the size of an avocado.

Did Mimi burn the paper? Was it on purpose? Or an accident? What did the paper say?

My head is so full of questions, I almost don't hear the rustle coming from behind the third dumpster. "Minerva?" I whisper.

Another rustle comes from the same spot.

I get to my feet and tiptoe toward the sound. I tiptoe closer and closer to where the rustle is coming from, turn the corner of the third dumpster, and . . .

A rat.

Not a metaphorical rat, like my sister, who sneaks around and hides things, but a real and true rat. The rat is brown and fat with a tail as long as a pom-pom string. The rat sniffs a hunk of meatloaf that has fallen from the dumpster. Then its whiskers move up and down as it nibbles.

I run for the exit door. I feel the rat crawling up my ankles and nibbling at my skin. I rush inside and slam the door shut. I'm shaking all over. I brush my hand across my ankles to wipe away the memory. The rat isn't on me, was never on me, but it feels like the rat will always be on me. It feels like the rat will be inside my head and part of my ankles forever.

I'm wrapping my arms around myself when I hear, "Bag? Is that you?"

I look up.

Mrs. Yoh.

She's standing near the swinging doors, holding a clipboard.

"What are you doing?" she asks.

I'm so upset, I'm not able to respond. It feels like if I open my mouth, the rat is going to jump inside.

"Well, come on," she says. "Let's check back with the girls. I was looking for Minerva. Oh my, I hope she finished that cheer!" Mrs. Yoh pushes the swinging doors open and looks left and right, seeing if anyone is in eyesight. No one is there.

"Let's put a little pep in our step," she says.

She rushes back to the storage closet. The entire time she talks, I stay several feet behind her.

She says, "The boys have a big game tomorrow, and a new cheer will be so inspiring. Oh my, I hope Minerva incorporates the word 'playoffs' into her writing. But then again, who am I to complain? Did Madonna, Prince, Boy George . . . Did any of the greats put the word 'playoffs' in their music? I think not. Genius, Bag, that's what your sister has. Genius."

Genius? Mrs. Yoh sure gets excited about cheerleading. I wonder if she was a cheerleader when she was in school. I wonder how she could still like it so much. She scoots down the hallways in quick, little steps.

In a daze, I continue to follow Mrs. Yoh. My mind is circling, and my stomach is in knots. We turn the corner, and before we get to the storage closet, we see the cheerleaders in the gym. Minerva is there too. She's surrounded by cheerleaders. She has a piece of paper in her hand. Mimi is next to her.

Mrs. Yoh rushes into the gym, rushes to Minerva. I follow.

"Oh, Minerva! There you are, dear. Did you finish the new cheer?"

Minerva hands Mrs. Yoh the piece of paper.

Mrs. Yoh looks over the new cheer. "Oh my word! This is absolutely wonderful, Minerva."

At the same time, Minerva narrows her eyes at me.

I narrow my eyes back at her.

"Girls!" Mrs. Yoh waves the cheer in her hand. "Let's work on this right away!"

The cheerleaders gather around Mrs. Yoh. She directs them to stand in two lines with Minerva at the center of the first line.

Before they begin the cheer, Mrs. Yoh turns to me. I'm standing off to the side. "Now, Bag, can you please help us with those pom-poms? They still need to be untangled."

I look at Mrs. Yoh.

Then I look at Minerva. She shakes her head.

I look back at Mrs. Yoh.

"Come to think of it, Bag, the speakers also need to be set up. Do you think you could stay for the rest of practice?"

I look at Minerva again. Her eyes burn daggers into mine. She mouths, "No."

My eyes return to Mrs. Yoh.

Mrs. Yoh crosses her fingers. "Please stay."

I keep my eyes on Mrs. Yoh, smile, and say, "I'd be happy to help."

"Wonderful!" She places a hand on her heart and says, "Girls, let me introduce you to our new equipment manager, Bag!"

chapter twelve-plus-one

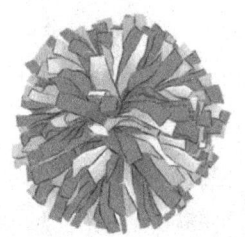

SO I STAY WITH THE CHEERLEADERS AND PRETEND I'm happy with the new position. I untangle pom-poms. I set up foam mats. I sync the speakers. I do everything expected of an equipment manager.

I also watch my sister.

Minerva doesn't do anything sneaky. She teaches the cheerleaders a new cheer called "Stealth." She runs it over and over and over with them. She makes up dance steps. She says she has an idea for a follow-up cheer.

Mrs. Yoh says, "Genius! That's what you are, Minerva. Genius!"

Mom picks us up on time. On the ride home not one thing about Minerva seems out of place. She hasn't done anything suspicious, not since her lie about going to the cafeteria. It's very frustrating. Minerva is being quiet and agreeable, like everything is fine. Everything is not fine. She was doing something sneaky when she said she was in the cafeteria.

Mom pulls her truck into the driveway. Minerva and Mom slide out. I reach for my backpack, which rests on the floor next to my feet. As I heave myself out of the truck, Minerva and Mom have already made their way into the house. I close the truck door and swing my backpack over my shoulder.

Then I hear a car rolling into the driveway. The car stops behind Mom's truck. By the sound of the sputtering engine and the smell of burnt rubber, I know exactly who the car belongs to. My dad.

He steps out of his old Honda. I notice his sunglasses first. On a cloudy afternoon, standing in the driveway, Dad wears black-rimmed sunglasses. He doesn't take them off when I wave.

Dad trudges toward me with a slight limp. The glasses cover the top half of his face. I notice that the corner of his sunglasses are crooked and the hinge thingy is held together with a small safety pin.

When Dad reaches me, he winces, shifts his weight onto his other foot.

"Dad! I didn't know you were coming," I say. It's been over two months since I saw him. Mom said he's been getting settled into his new place.

I'm so, so happy to see him, and want to ask him so

many questions, but I pause. I want to ask him about his new place, but I don't want him to think I'm happy about him moving out. I want him back in our house. So I don't bring up the new place at all.

"Happy to be of service," he says.

He winces again.

"Your knee?" I ask.

"Aw, it'll be all right." He gives his leg a tap. "Just a little rusty from the weather. All these clouds make it ache."

"I'm sorry your knee hurts."

He nods. "Your Mom said I could swing by and pick you up."

"She didn't say anything to me." I look back at the house. Mom's standing in the window. Her mouth stays frowning. Why didn't she tell me he was coming?

Dad rubs his stubbly chin. "Want to go ask? Make sure it's still all right?"

"That's okay, Dad. I'm sure it's fine." There's no way I'm going to ask her permission. I've been waiting to see Dad for weeks. I can't wait to be in his car, to roll down the window, to talk about nature and music and all the good things in the world. There's no way she's going to take that away from me.

I should probably see if Minerva wants to come with us, but I doubt she'll want to. She despises Dad's car. Plus, it'll hurt Dad's feelings if she says no. Tonight, I realize, I'm getting my dad all to myself, which is the best thing ever.

So, without saying another word, I slide into the front seat of Dad's Honda. The beige carpet has a brown stain. The carpet also has vacuum lines as if maybe Dad tried to tidy up but no matter how much he vacuumed, the stain wouldn't go away.

Dad closes my door, more creaking and squeaking. I watch him in the rearview mirror. He shuffles to the other side of the car, gets behind the wheel, and starts the engine.

The Doobie Brothers blast from the car stereo. The phrase "It keeps you running, yeah, it keeps you running" plays over and over.

Dad taps the base of his hand against the steering wheel. "I love this song."

"Yeah," I say. "I remember."

Random Thought 510
It's been over two months since I saw my dad, eleven months since Mom made him move out of our house. Based on the way he's acting, numbers don't count for much.

The Doobie Brothers keep singing, and Dad backs out of the driveway. The windows of his car are rolled down, which I love.

"Man," Dad says. "These guys know how to do it."

"Do what?"

"Listen to the lyrics."

The Doobie Brothers repeat the line about running. They say "running" a lot. So much that I'm beginning to think it's the only line of the song.

"It's about running," I say.

"You've really got to listen." Dad moves his head back and forth with the music. "It's about a girl who's having a hard time and she's running away, and those Doobies, man, they understand. Those Doobies, they've got soul. They know running ain't gonna fix nothin'."

"I hear you," I say.

"Your Mom called. Said she got a part in a play."

"Yeah," I say.

"Said she couldn't take you to the library."

"Yeah," I say.

Dad nods his head in rhythm to the music. "Want to go to the library now?"

"It's closed."

"Aw, Maggie. I'm sorry."

For the first time in a long time, it feels like someone understands. Dad sure is good with his words, aside from his thoughts about the Doobie Brothers. The Doobies keep singing. Dad keeps driving. Finally he pulls into Scoops-n-Stuff, my favorite place to get ice cream.

"Thanks," I say.

"You got it," he says.

He turns down the music and stops at the drive-through. An excited voice calls from the intercom, "Welcome to Scoops-n-Stuff! If we don't put a smile on your face, no sweet treat will!"

The ice cream is really good here even though the slogan is ridiculous.

Dad leans toward the intercom. "Hi, darlin'."

Funny, the ice cream lady got a *Hi, darlin'* from him, whereas I got a Doobie Brothers song.

"What can I get you?" the voice says, super high-pitched as if the lady is about to eat ice cream rather than scoop it. Come to think of it, maybe she's already taken a taste? She sure sounds like she's had a lot of sugar today.

Dad turns to me. "Still like vanilla?"

"Yeah," I say.

Dad leans toward the intercom. "A small vanilla shake and a large mocha surprise with extra chocolate syrup and sprinkles."

"Great!" she says. "That'll be . . . nine dollars and thirteen cents."

"Twelve-plus-one," Dad corrects her.

She giggles. "Also known as 'thirteen.'"

"It's a bad-luck, no-good number," he says.

"For real?" she asks.

"You ever been on a boat?" he replies.

A boat? What's my dad talking about?

As if reading my mind, she asks, "What's a boat got to do with anything?"

"Say that number on a boat, you'd better jump off because, mark my words, that ship's sinking."

I stare at Dad. Doesn't he know how old I am? Does he have any idea I'm about to turn his least-favorite number?

Dad tenses his jaw, thinking about the number thirteen. I squirm in my seat and decide to keep my upcoming age to myself.

Another giggle comes from the intercom. "Pull up to the window," the ice cream lady says.

Dad clicks the gearshift into drive, and the tires of his Honda roll across gravel.

We pull up to the window, and there's a lady with a pink visor, a pretty face, and a high ponytail that swings to the left. She looks Dad's age, maybe older, which is surprising, since I didn't know adult women wore their hair in high side ponies. I also didn't know adult women giggled.

Come to think of it, all the women who work at Scoops-n-Stuff are pretty and laugh with a high voice. Maybe Scoops-n-Stuff asks them to greet people that way? Maybe Scoops-n-Stuff wants their employees to sound like the slogan? *If we don't put a smile on your face, no sweet treat will!*

I think Scoops-n-Stuff would be way better if they

got rid of the slogan. I mean, it's ice cream. Ice cream sells itself.

"Hi!" she says, still with the excited voice. "That'll be nine dollars and twelve-plus-one cents, please."

Dad keeps his glasses on, shifts forward, and reaches into the back pocket of his jeans. He pulls out a bunch of singles, no wallet, and I watch him count ten dollars.

Random Thought 332
I wish Dad didn't pay for my shake. If
he's worried about money, the last thing
he needs is for me to take more away.

Dad passes the wrinkled singles through the window, and now that he's in the presence of the ice cream lady, he's quiet and awkward, like it's easier for him to talk to her through the intercom than face-to-face.

The lady holds out two shakes. "Here you go!"

He reaches for the shakes.

"Have a day filled with sunshine and rainbows!" she says.

"We won't," I mumble, because, when you think about it, that's impossible. Sunshine means clear skies. Rainbows only happen when sunshine mixes with clouds.

Dad pulls away from the window and parks under a big maple tree. With his teeth he pulls off the straw's wrapper and spits it into the cup holder. The cup holder is filled with loose change, a used Band-Aid, and a white plastic token that says EASY DOES IT.

Then Dad shoves the straw into the straw hole and guzzles down his mocha surprise. As for me, I don't take a sip of my shake. I'm too busy thinking about my dad. What's his new place like? What's he been doing there? Why hasn't he come to visit sooner? I want to ask him these questions, but I'm worried about how he might answer. What if he doesn't like his new place? What if he hasn't been busy? What if he didn't want to visit?

Dad glances over at me holding my shake, not drinking it.

"New glasses?" he asks.

I touch my index finger against the red frame resting on the bridge of my nose. "Same pair. I've had them for a long time."

"They suit you," he says.

"Thanks," I whisper, and feel like a phony.

Dad doesn't know that the glasses aren't real. Dad doesn't know I have dyslexia. When the doctor told Mom, my parents were fighting all the time. It was in New York, and Mom's soap, *The Rich and the Radiant*, had just been canceled. She was constantly mad at Dad. I'm sure she didn't tell him about my dyslexia or my fake glasses.

I wanted to tell him back then, when I went to the

doctor, but I didn't want to give him even more to worry about. Mom was so mad when her soap was canceled. Dad was tiptoeing around the apartment, like he didn't want to disturb her, or us, or anything. I figured me and my doctor visit, my stupid dyslexia, would sink the whole ship.

I really want to tell him now. I want to tell Dad the truth, holding our shakes from Scoops-n-Stuff. I want to tell him because it's bad to keep a secret from someone you love. So I take off my glasses and use the bottom of my T-shirt to rub the plain glass clean. "Dad?" I start to say.

But the words won't leave my mouth.

I swallow, and my throat is dry and tight, like that awful hot air from Mom's truck has found a way inside me. I shift uncomfortably in the passenger seat of the Honda and keep my mouth shut.

I can't tell Dad, because there's no way I want to say the truth about my dyslexia. There's no way I want him to know I'm not smart. After all, Dad's the only person in our family who says I am smart. I don't want him to change his mind about me. I mean, it's bad enough I'm about to turn his least-favorite number.

"Everything okay?" he asks.

"Sure," I say. "Thanks again for picking me up, even if we couldn't go to the library."

I put the glasses back onto my face.

Dad takes another swig of his shake. Then he picks

up his EASY DOES IT token and rubs it with the tip of his thumb. I wonder where he got the token. It looks like something from an arcade or a sports bar. Is the place near here? Is it called Easy Does It? He tosses the token back into the cup holder. It seems like my dad is thinking about something, like me, and maybe he doesn't want to say it out loud either.

"Let's get back," he finally says.

He heads in the direction we came from. We're in the car, drinking our shakes, with the music turned up. We pass by a house with pink flamingos in the yard. We pass by a house with the lights turned off. We pass by a house with a dying tree in front. The Doobie Brothers keep singing about dancing and rivers and castles and feeling happy.

> **Random Thought 781.1**
>
> I wish the Doobie Brothers were singing about something different, like a song about a broken bike, or a sickly cat, or a lonely old house. It would feel better than pretending everything is fine.

chapter fourteen

DAD PULLS UP TO THE HOUSE. THERE'S A bunch of cars in the driveway. I see Mom's old truck, a little yellow convertible, and a Volvo.

"Looks like a party," Dad says.

I can't believe she invited people over. She never invites people over. Now Dad's going to think she has people over all the time. He's going to think the house is happy and good and full of people. He's going to think nobody misses him. I can't believe my mother would do this.

"It's not a party," I say to Dad. "Mom doesn't have parties."

Dad nods. He's still wearing his sunglasses. Which seems strange, seeing how it's dark outside. He doesn't need the sunglasses. I realize we're a lot alike, me and my dad. I wear reading glasses to feel smart, because I know I'm not. Maybe Dad wears sunglasses to feel cool, because he's worried he isn't.

We pull over and park on the street. Dad pushes his hand through his hair and scratches the top of his head. With a hand on his head, the sleeve of his windbreaker moves up, and I see a small, white sticker in the shape of a square on the inside part of his forearm. He sighs and places his hand back on the steering wheel.

I motion toward his arm. "What's that?"

He looks down. "Last thing I got to kick," he says. "The cigarettes."

"Do you need steps for that, too?"

"Yeah," he sighs. "I do."

> **Random Thought 178**
> When adults drink too much or smoke too much or shop too much or eat too much, there are steps you can take to stop. I don't know what the steps are, but they must be really smart to make someone act like a completely new person.

Dad takes off his sunglasses and, without folding them up, places them on the dashboard. I wonder if the little safety pin makes them impossible to fold? He rubs the bridge of his nose. Then he looks at me. His brown eyes are warm, the color of a chocolate Lab, the same color as mine. Is he trying to show me his real self? Is that why he took off his sunglasses?

I want to show him my real self too.

So I say, "You know that number? Thirteen?"

Dad grimaces.

"Sorry," I say. "I mean twelve-plus-one."

Dad shakes his head. "It's a no-good number."

I bite my bottom lip before I ask, "So, you know how my birthday is on the twenty-ninth?"

Dad's face freezes, and then he nods. As he nods, he looks like he remembered that my birthday is on the twenty-ninth. But that frozen second makes me think he forgot. But that doesn't matter. Whether he remembers my birthday isn't important. What's important is that I need his advice.

"Dad, when my birthday comes around, should I pretend I'm fourteen so I don't have to be . . ." I pause. I don't want to say his least-favorite number. "Or should I just tell people I'm twelve-plus-one?"

"Aw, Maggie." Dad rubs the stubble on his face. "My sweet girl." He looks right at me. His warm brown eyes are full of understanding. "You should always say what you are." He rubs the top of my head and then pulls his hand away. "You're turning just the right number. Nothing to worry about."

"When were you on a boat?" I ask.

"Never," he says.

"How do you know it'll sink?"

"Stories, Maggie."

"Stories?" I ask excitedly. "Stories from books?"

Dad shakes his head.

"Do you still have your books?" I ask. "From our apartment in New York? Do you read them? Are there books in your new place?"

I didn't mean to ask all those questions. They just kind of poured out.

Dad smiles. "I forgot how much you love books." He gives the top of my head a little pat. "I'm talking about stories from my friends."

"Oh."

"We sit in circles. We tell stories. I trust them."

"Got it," I say. "I'll tell people I'm twelve-plus-one."

Dad nods. Even though we don't say it, I think we both know I'm turning a no-good number.

This idea sends a chill across my body. I pretend I'm in my own little circle with my dad. I want him to trust me, like he trusts his friends, so I say another true thing.

"Minerva's up to something."

"What do you mean?"

"I'm not sure, but I'm going to find out."

"Aw, she's a good kid. Your sister's got fire in her

blood, and there's nothing wrong with a little temper. She's got a lot to be mad about."

"Yeah, but . . ." I feel my own blood heat up. We all have a lot to be mad about, but that doesn't mean it's okay to treat people like garbage. "Minerva is all about Minerva."

The moment I say it, I want to take it back because it's a snarky thing to say, especially about my sister, even though it's the truth.

"Fair enough," Dad says. Then he turns up the Doobie Brothers. The Doobies sing about *eyes* and *silver* and *rubies* and *diamonds*. I reach for the car door's handle.

I open the door and step outside. My head is like a bathtub filled to the brim with water and the faucet keeps running. Oh god. I realize my head is like a Doobie Brothers song. *It keeps you running, yeah, it keeps you running.* Water splashes over the sides of my brain, and I think about Minerva and Mimi, the burnt paper, the dumpsters, and the little burn hole in my sister's cheerleading skirt.

"See you," he says.

"See you," I say back.

Dad smiles, a nice, broad smile, and I want to ask him to stay. Even though it would be weird to have him in the house and Minerva would be furious and Mom would be uncomfortable, I want to ask him in.

"I've got to go," he says in a way that tells me he doesn't want me to ask him in. So I shut the door. Dad gives a honk and pulls away from the curb. His Honda rambles down the darkening street. I realize I don't know where he's going. I don't even know where he lives.

Night air nips at my earlobes and face and neck and hands. It touches every part of my uncovered skin. I feel numb, like my overflowing tub has frozen and the water that was spurting from the faucet hangs as still as an icicle in the bathroom of a tiny apartment. I wonder if the Doobie Brothers have a song about that.

chapter fifteen

ON THE STOOP OF MY HOUSE, WITH MY HAND on the doorknob, I hear people singing.

"He had it coming, he had it coming, he only had himself to blame . . ." Two female voices harmonize in perfect pitch.

A male voice interrupts. "Let's do *Hamilton*!"

"Yes, Carl!" a female voice says. "*Hamilton!* Go!"

"Alexander Hamilton. My name is Alexander Hamilton."

His voice is strong and clear and in tune. I lean to the left and peek through the window next to the front door. The living room is empty. The singing comes from the kitchen. Why are people singing inside my house?

"When he was ten, his father split, full of it, debt-ridden . . ."

I slowly open the front door. I creep toward the singing and turn the corner into our tiny kitchen. Two strangers are standing at the counter. One woman. One man. They're chopping cucumbers, stacking chicken kebobs, and packing shortbread cookies into Tupperware. The man faces the sink and keeps singing. His voice sounds like Lin-Manuel Miranda's but deeper and raspier, like a blues singer or, dare I say, the Doobie Brothers.

I've never seen these people in my life.

Mom's standing near the kitchen table. She faces the strangers with her back turned away from me. She has no idea I'm here.

The man stops singing, still standing near the sink.

"Lenore," he says, "how about a duet?"

"Yes!" Mom says. *"Grease!"* She whips her arms out to the sides, does a little dance move, turns around, and sees me. "Oh, Bag!" Her eyes meet mine. Her arms are still extended out. "I didn't know you were home!" She doesn't move her arms, which looks awkward. I can't tell if she stays frozen like that because she's surprised to see me or because I'm interrupting the *Grease* song.

Random Thought 809.7

I despise the movie *Grease*. At the end the lady changes herself for no good reason. She sheds her pink tube skirt for a tight black jumpsuit. She smokes and smirks and acts tough. She changes herself because she's in love with John Travolta and she wants John Travolta to love her back. In my opinion it's a terrible story. If you ask my mom, it's the absolute best.

"Come and sing with us!" Mom holds her hand out to me.

I do not take her hand.

"Summer lovin', had me a blast," she sings.

"Mom," I say.

"Summer lovin', happened so fast," the man sings.

"Mom," I say.

She ignores me, and they keep going. My mom croons, "Summer days drifting away . . ."

"Stop!" I shout.

She finally stops singing and looks at me. I feel my heart heating up and sending hot blood to my face, which I'm certain is bright red. I didn't mean to shout. It's just that, well, I really want them to stop singing.

"Oh gosh," she says. "I guess I got a bit carried away. Bag, I'd like to introduce you to my friends." She motions to the man and the woman. "These are my friends from the play, Carl and Cynthia." Mom puts her hand on my shoulder. "Guys, this is my daughter Bag."

"Love your name," Cynthia says.

"Couldn't agree more," Carl says.

Cynthia asks me, "Do kids actually eat this?" She holds up a large red bowl filled with cucumbers and yogurt.

I shrug. "I don't."

"It's raita," Mom explains. "Kids love it. They use it as a dip," Mom points to the other end of the counter. "For the chicken kebobs."

Cynthia begins to stir what's in the bowl.

Mom motions to Cynthia. "Bag," she says, "Cynthia is also in the play. She's fabulous."

"Oh, Lenore. Thank you!" Then Cynthia points to the handwritten notes on our kitchen wall. "Are these yours?"

"Moi?" Mom smiles.

"Mais oui," says Carl.

"But of course," Mom says.

"How creative," Cynthia says.

"Mom." I put my hands on my hips. This party is the worst idea ever. She knew Dad was coming over. Why isn't she asking about him? Why did she invite these people here? Why is she in such a good mood? Dad just left!

I stare at her and narrow my eyes. "It's a school night. There shouldn't be a party here on school nights. And why didn't you come out and say hi to Dad?"

"Oh, sweetheart. This isn't a party. Cynthia and Carl

came over to help." Mom goes back to her piece of paper on the table. "It was a nightmare at school today. A nut allergy." Mom clutches her heart. "Not a dreaded nut allergy!" Then her dramatic voice changes to a plain one. "I'm still not convinced it was from my meal. Needless to say, I got called out of rehearsal to deal with the allergy, and they kept me there forever. And then my friends came over to help prep while I ran out to get Tupperware."

Mom turns to her new friends. She doesn't bring up Dad at all. It's so annoying. "You met Cynthia," she says. "She plays my daughter in the play. And this is Carl. He plays my homeless husband."

Her daughter? Her homeless husband? Cynthia and Mom look the same age, so I have no idea why they are playing mother and daughter. On the other hand, Carl looks a lot younger than Mom, and he's supposed to be her husband? If you ask me, it looks like someone really messed up the casting.

"Her homeless husband!" Cynthia says. "Ha!"

"It's brilliant," Carl says. "The show is brilliant. You are brilliant, Cynthia. You are brilliant, Lenore. This story belongs onstage."

"Oh, Carl," says Cynthia. "Your talent astounds me. Both of you." She turns to Mom. "Your talent astounds me."

These people make my stomach queasy. They've

given and received more compliments in the past five minutes than I've given and received in my whole life.

Speaking of a person who loves getting compliments.

"Where's Minerva?" I ask.

"She went with you and your dad. Didn't she?" Finally she wants to talk about Dad.

"Why didn't you tell me he was coming?" I ask. "He said he called you. He said you talked about it. Why didn't you tell me?"

"Oh, sweetheart, I didn't want you to be disappointed. In case he didn't show up."

"He did show up, Mom," I say in a very serious voice. "So you were wrong about him. And no, Minerva didn't come with us."

The wrinkles on Mom's forehead deepen. "What do you mean? Minerva said she would. After I saw you and your father in the window, she said she was meeting you in the driveway."

"Nope," I say. "She didn't."

Mom quickly turns to her new friends. "Hold down the fort. I'll be right back."

"Oh, Captain, my captain." Carl stands up on a chair, and I feel the sudden urge to yank the chair out from under him just to see if he lands on his feet.

"Raita?" Cynthia asks. "Or raito?"

Carl says, "Take as much time as you need, Lenore. We can finish up here."

Random Thought 790.2

Theater people: Love to sing. Love to compliment each other. Love to be packed into small spaces with other theater people. Love to help.

Mom rushes to Minerva's room. I follow because I have a sneaking suspicion that Minerva isn't there. She probably ran away because she didn't want to be in a car with me and Dad.

Mom speeds down the hall, and I stay at her heels. I picture Minerva's spotless room, her bare desk, her perfectly made bed, and her cheerleading banner. I picture the room without Minerva inside.

"Minerva?" Mom says. Minerva's door is closed. Mom knocks twice.

Minerva doesn't respond.

"Minerva?" Mom opens the door.

Turns out I'm wrong. Minerva didn't run away. She's in her room. She's sitting on her bed hunched over a large stack of papers. Her pink-and-peach bedspread is neatly tucked in at the corners.

"Minerva," Mom says.

Minerva doesn't look at her.

"Minerva, I asked you . . ."

"Don't care." Minerva keeps her attention on her homework.

Mom sighs and turns to leave. But before she walks through Minerva's door, she whips back around. The wrinkle lines in her forehead are super deep. She has a smudge of yogurt on her cheek.

"I'm doing the best I can!" Mom shouts.

Minerva shifts on her bed and looks at her. Mom is trembling, and she puts her arms around herself. At the same time, Minerva bites her bottom lip. Tears well up in the bottoms of her eyes, but she doesn't let any fall out.

"Look," Mom says in a gentle voice. "It's been a day. There was a nut allergy at school, and I needed help with tomorrow's meal, and I was really hoping you would take a drive with your dad. You told me you were going."

"Whatever," Minerva says. "I changed my mind."

I can't believe it. Mom is being way too easy on Minerva. She lied right to her face!

"Minerva." Mom takes a breath. "I understand. I understand maybe you didn't want to go. I just wish you would've talked to me about it."

"I was busy," my sister says.

"Busy?" I mumble. "Busy with what?"

She doesn't answer my question. Instead she says, "Who are the freaks in the kitchen—"

Mom cuts in. "My friends from the play. Would you like to meet them?"

"The guy has a good voice. The one singing the song from *Grease*," she says. "I love that movie."

"Me too!" Mom exclaims. "You can sing with us! You've got a great voice, Minerva."

Minerva shifts her legs off the bed and then changes her mind. She looks at the stack of math sheets spread across her bed and tucks her legs back into a cross-legged position. "Can't. Too much homework. Plus, there's a game tomorrow."

Too much homework? Minerva usually finishes her homework faster than fast.

"It's a playoff game," Minerva says. "Are you going?"

"I'm going to the game," I say.

Minerva gives me a horrible look. Her nostrils flare and her eyes turn into slits. "I was talking to Mom."

"I'll see what I can do about the game," Mom says. Then she raises her eyebrows at me and Minerva, and her wrinkles go even deeper. "Love you both."

"Love you too," I mumble.

Minerva doesn't say anything.

Mom goes back to the kitchen, and I'm beyond annoyed. Mom's being so nice to Minerva even though I was the one who went with Dad and Minerva was the one who lied about going because she was *busy*. I inch toward Minerva on her bed. Something isn't right. What was she *busy* doing?

On her bed she's holding a pencil. There's a worksheet in front of her. I notice she's wearing a ring on her pointer finger. The ring is turquoise and gold and beautiful.

"Where did you get that?"

She slams her hand on top of the sheet.

"The ring," I say.

"I don't know," she replies.

She keeps her hand on the sheet, and I see that the sheet is filled with math problems. Long division. It looks like the same homework I got today from Mrs. Buttocks. "Why are you doing seventh-grade math?" I ask.

"You little creep!" Minerva slams the stack of papers face down on her bed. "Stop spying on me."

"Why didn't you want to see Dad?" I ask.

"I—" Minerva looks at me, and for the tiniest moment I feel like she actually wants to be my friend. She looks at me and she doesn't look away, and it's like she's about to tell me something. "It's just that—"

"You can trust me," I say. "What?"

"Ugh," Minerva says. "Just go away."

"Minerva."

"Go!" she screams.

Fine. I tried to be cool. I tried to talk to her. But if she's just going to be mean, I'm going to get the truth out of her one way or another.

"Why does your skirt have a burn hole?" I ask.

"Get out of my room."

"Why were you at the dumpsters?"

"Go."

"Where did you get that ring?"

"LEAVE!" Minerva chucks a pillow at my head.

I duck. Then I run for the hallway. I slam the door behind me, and the hinges click into place. At the same time, an idea clicks inside my head. I think I know. I think I know what my sister's hiding.

> **Random Thought 364**
>
> I've got to be smart about this. Minerva is sensitive. Minerva is private. Minerva doesn't like to be wrong. Even though I want to interrogate my sister with my suspicions, I've got to hold them in. I've got to hold them in until I catch her in the act.

After I complete my math homework, eat dinner with Mom and her new theater friends, listen to Carl sing Miss Hannigan from *Annie*, say good night, get into my pajamas, and crawl under my covers, I'm exhausted.

I think about reading.

I'm not even halfway through *The Old Man and the Sea* and I've got two other classics lined up, *A Wrinkle in Time* and *Little Women*, but my chances of finishing *The Old Man and the Sea* by the end of the week are nonexistent. At this point people who don't even like books read more than me. I've got to get my act together. I slap my cheeks and pick up *The Old Man and the Sea*.

There was cast net boy remembering went . . . pot of yellow rice fish . . .

My eyes are doing the weird thing when they take forever to translate the letters to my brain. I'm frustrated and I close the book. My dyslexia always creeps up when I'm tired. Or when I have to read in front of people. Or when I have to figure out my right from my left. I guess my dyslexia creeps up a lot.

My eyelids grow heavier and heavier, and I don't have the energy to take off my glasses and rub the bridge of my nose. So I set *The Old Man and the Sea* on my chest, close my eyes, and turn off my busted brain.

chapter sixteen

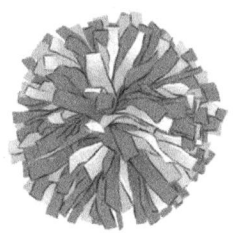

THE NEXT MORNING WE'RE BACK IN THE TRUCK, me, Mom, and Minerva. Once again I'm stuck in the middle seat. Once again I'd prefer the window. Mom sings loudly. I think it's a Taylor Swift song.

"It's new, the shape of your body. It's blue, the feeling I've got . . ."

Her singing makes me think of Dad and his Doobie Brothers. She loves the song, the same way Dad loves his Doobies.

Random Thought 173
Most of the time I don't understand why my parents got married. They're total opposites. Except, when they aren't being opposites, they seem perfect for each other.

"Seriously, Mom." Minerva knocks her head against the window. "For the love of everything normal, please stop singing."

Mom stops and sighs. The truck becomes quiet. After a few moments of no singing, Mom clears her throat. Then she puckers her lips and lifts her chin, like she did on *The Rich and the Radiant* right before the camera started rolling.

"Life is a drama full of tragedy and comedy. You should learn to enjoy the comic episodes a little more," Mom says.

"Huh," I say.

Mom faces the road, but it feels like she's talking to me.

"Are you saying I should be funnier?" I ask.

Mom stays looking at the road, her hands gripping the steering wheel. "No, sweetheart. It's a line," she says. "From the play."

"Weird. It sounds like what you'd say in real life."

She continues. "You should never hate anyone, even your worst enemies. Everyone has something good about them. You have to find the redeeming quality and love the person for that."

"Everyone has something good about them. I like that," I say. "Is that line from the play too?"

"Sure is," Mom says. "How do I sound?"

"Like yourself."

"Wonderful."

"Aren't you supposed to sound like an actor?"

"Absolutely not," she says. "I want to sound natural."

"Ugh," Minerva groans from the window seat. "Can you stop already with the lines?"

"Nothing wrong with practicing, Minerva." Mom keeps her eyes on the road.

Minerva says, "Are you going to the game tonight?"

"Oh gosh, that's right, sweetheart. The game. It's just that we have our first full run-through tonight. We're going to go through the entire play, start to finish. I really need to be there. But I can definitely pick you up after. And Bag."

"Bag is not going to the game," Minerva says.

"Actually," I say to Mom, "I am. Mrs. Yoh asked me to help."

"Oh my stars. I knew it! Baggie as a cheerleader!"

"Why are you so excited about Bag?" Minerva asks.

"I'm not a cheerleader," I tell Mom. "I'm the equipment manager."

Then, like a kettle of hot water boiling over, Minerva opens her mouth. "Bag is not the equipment manager. She does not belong there at all!"

"Take it easy, Minerva." Mom takes a hard right without using her blinker. "I think it's wonderful that Bag has found something to do after school."

"Lenore." Minerva's voice is sharp and snarky. "You've got to be kidding."

Mom grips the steering wheel. "Do not call me Lenore."

"Whatever you say, Lenore."

Oh no. It feels like Mom and Minerva are about to explode. I slump down in the middle seat so when they lose their tempers, the sound doesn't go directly into my ears.

"It's disrespectful," Mom says. "I'm your mother. I'm not Lenore to you."

Minerva doesn't call her Lenore again. The car stays uncomfortably quiet. I scrunch up in the awful middle seat and wait for Mom to pull up to school. She stops the truck at the curb, and Minerva jumps out. My sister heads to school without saying goodbye to us.

I jump out of the truck and keep my eyes on her. She heads toward the front steps of school. I watch her stop near the school entrance.

"See you in the gym," I tell Mom.

She blows me a kiss, and I rush to the entrance. I duck behind a large statue near the front steps, close to where Minerva is standing. The statue is an eagle taking flight, and I peek my nose out from one of the bronze wings. Minerva doesn't see me. She greets Emily C. and Emily S. with a smile and hugs.

"What's up?"

"Hi!"

"Totally."

The girls talk to each other as they hug. It doesn't make any sense to me.

Random Thought 304.8
Hugs shouldn't be treated like handshakes or hellos. Hugs are meaningful. Hugs should be saved for someone you care about. Because when you treat a hug like it's important, the person receiving the hug feels it.

Now Minerva is telling them a story. I stick my head farther out from the eagle's wing and catch a few words. ". . . so cringeworthy . . . sunglasses . . . gross." I'm pretty sure she's talking about Dad showing up in our driveway. She sounds embarrassed by him. Or embarrassed by me. Or, most likely, both of us.

"Bag?"

I hear my name before I know who says it. I turn to see a basketball player standing next to me. I think his name is Sheldon. Or Sherman. He's tall. I'm pretty sure he's the center on the basketball team.

"I heard you joined cheerleading," he says.

I shrug. "I'm the equipment manager."

"Cool," he says.

"I guess," I say.

At this point nothing feels cool about cheerleading.

Minerva keeps telling the cheerleaders a story. The cheerleaders laugh. I wonder if it's the same story about me and my dad.

Then the bell rings and the front door of school opens.

"So I guess you're working with your sister now."

"You mean at cheerleading?"

"Um . . ." He pauses. "Yeah, sure." He pauses again. Then he says, "See you."

"See you," I say.

The entire interaction is very weird. I still don't know if his name is Sheldon or Sherman. And why is he asking about Minerva?

I turn to watch Minerva link arms with her posse of cheerleaders. The girls head through the front entrance. Minerva leads the way. Mimi Fookwire is nowhere in sight. I step out from behind the eagle and—

"Ouch!"

Heads knock. A book drops. I look up. It's Ridgley.

I've been so caught up with Minerva and her friends and cheerleading, I forgot about Ridgley. I really want to go to the library with him. I wish I could've gone with him the other day.

I want to tell him that, that I want to hang out with him, but I feel weird. What if he doesn't want to hang out with me? Plus, I didn't plan on bumping into him, and I don't want to make things even weirder. So I look down. On the ground there's a slim book with a bookmark sticking out from the top. Seeing his book reminds me of my own reading list and how far behind I am with *The Old Man and the Sea*. *Get it together,* I tell myself.

I bend down and pick up Ridgley's book. It's another Chekhov play, *The Seagull*. "Do you like it?" I ask.

"Not really." Ridgley grabs the book from my hand. His mouth turns down, he grips the book, and his eyes keep shifting everywhere, except to me. I really want him to look at me. The bell rings again. We both stay put.

"It's the second bell," I say. "We'll be late."

Ridgley shakes his head. "I can't believe it, Margaret."

Can't believe what?

He shakes his head again, like, *Come on*, I should know. Is he talking about me going to cheerleading instead of the library?

"I wanted to go to the library," I say.

"Really?" he replies. "I hear you're a cheerleader now."

"I'm not a cheerleader," I say. "I'm the equipment manager."

He holds my gaze.

Then, without any explanation, Ridgley turns, walks away, and leaves me standing in front of the school, alone.

chapter seventeen

A PAIN THE SIZE OF A PLUM ACHES IN THE MIDDLE of my body.

It feels so awful that I hunch over near the school's front entrance. The front steps are packed. People rush past. I wish everyone could see how much my insides are hurting. Maybe they'd be more careful. Maybe they'd give me space.

But they don't.

I hear loud sounds. Someone shoves my backpack. Not one person notices I'm not okay. Not one person notices I'm hunched over.

I take a deep breath. Why did Ridgley leave me like that? Is he mad at me? I'm not a cheerleader!

I feel awful and try to stand up straight, step one foot in front of the other. I walk up the front steps, through the door, across the hall. I reach my locker and turn the combination. Four, fourteen, twenty. It doesn't open. Four, fourteen, twenty. It still won't open.

I slam my hand against the locker door, and the person standing next to me says, "Take it easy."

He's an eighth grader, a basketball player. I don't know his name, but he looks like a Cody or a Brody or something that sounds cool.

"What are you doing to Anna Beth's locker?" he wants to know.

"Anna Beth?" I mumble.

I look at the locker. It's got a dent at the bottom. Next to the dent, a sticker that says PUNK. Oh no. It's not my locker. I'm at the wrong locker. I'm not even in the seventh-grade wing.

"You trying to steal her stuff?" he says.

"No," I say.

The eighth graders gather around us. My head spins and spins. I want to get away. I didn't mean to do anything wrong. I start to sprint down the hall. My heart beats as fast as a hamster running on a well-greased wheel. My backpack smashes against my lower spine and something pointy digs into my tailbone. *The Old Man and the Sea!* I slow my pace because I don't want to hurt the library book. Or myself.

When I reach the cafeteria, I look through the window next to the double doors. Inside, everything is empty and clean. The quiet room gives me a moment to pause. Even under terrible circumstances, I've got a book in my backpack. I've got this good, quiet room in front of me. No matter what happens, nobody can take that away from me.

Random Thought 131
When life is awful, sometimes you've got to make your own magic.

I'm about to move past the cafeteria to my first class when, out the corner of my eye, I see her. Mimi. She comes through the exit door in the back corner of the cafeteria—the door that leads to the dumpsters.

Now. Now is my chance. Maybe Minerva won't tell me what's going on, but I'll get it out of Mimi. "Oh hey," I say as if it's a total coincidence that I'm headed into the cafeteria at the exact moment she's coming out.

"Bag."

"Mimi."

"I don't want to be late," she says. She clutches a manila folder.

Before she leaves the cafeteria, I say, "Last night's math homework was hard, huh?"

"Yeah." She shifts the folder in her hand. "I mean, sort of, I guess, not really?"

My theory is totally coming together. "Mimi, are your parents smokers?"

"Smokers?"

"Do they smoke cigarettes?"

"My mom does. So?"

"Do you?"

"Gross. No!"

"Thanks for the information," I say.

"What information?"

"See you at cheerleading," I say.

Mimi pinches her lips together, and her tiny face looks even smaller than usual. "See you," she says in a squeaky voice. Then she rushes down the hallway still clutching that manila folder.

chapter eighteen

AFTER A TERRIBLE SPANISH CLASS, AN OKAY science class, and life skills, I've now got Buttocks for fourth period, I'm seconds away from being late, and my math book is still in my locker. I've got two options.

Option one. Go to my locker, which will make me late and I'll get a tardy slip. Option two. Don't go to my locker, I won't have my math book, and I'll get yelled at by Mrs. Buttocks.

Random Thought 808.7
It's a lose-lose situation.

I run past my locker without stopping to grab my math book because I don't want a tardy slip. Tardy slips are the worst. There's no way I want to see my name on the bright yellow sheet that says I'm late, I'm a mess, I'm just no good. I already know this is true, so why would I want to see it on a bright yellow piece of paper?

I turn the corner and sprint to class. Hopefully, Mrs. Buttocks won't notice my lack of a math book. Maybe we'll have a fire drill or a visit from the principal, or maybe she'll send me to the nurse for a lice check. Fingers crossed!

Mimi is a few feet ahead of me. She's holding a manila folder. Is it the same folder from this morning? I wonder what's inside it. I follow Mimi, and the clock in the hallway ticks to the cadence of our footsteps. Any second now . . . four, three, two . . .

The late bell blasts above us, and we shuffle into Mrs. Buttocks's classroom, barely on time. Before I close the door, I see Ridgley. He's watching me from across the hall.

"What did I do?" I mouth.

He shakes his head.

"Girls," Mrs. Buttocks's shrill voice whips me around to face the classroom. "For the last time, take your seats."

Mimi jumps into the desk in front of mine. I stumble after. I can't see Ridgley across the hallway, but I'm still thinking about him. Why is he ignoring me? It's the absolute worst feeling.

"Attention, everyone." Mrs. Buttocks stands in front of the classroom. She wears a sweater the color of diarrhea.

"It has been brought to my attention that our test

scores are below grade level." Mrs. Buttocks walks between the rows of desks and continues to speak. "This is unacceptable. Unacceptable!"

She keeps walking between the rows and pauses when she gets to my desk. "And yet day after day your homework is above grade level, which leads me to believe . . ." She's standing in front of the classroom now. "It must be test anxiety."

Mimi shoves her folder into her backpack.

"How many of you are anxious taking tests?" Mrs. Buttocks asks.

Every person in class shoots a hand into the air. I follow with my own hand because, seriously, who isn't anxious taking a test? I'm surprised she even needs to ask.

"I had a feeling you'd raise your hands," she says in a clipped voice. "You can put your hands down because I'm certain it's more than anxiety going on."

The class follows her orders.

"I'm curious if some of you are getting help with your homework? From a parent? Or an older sibling?"

"Yeah, right," I whisper. Minerva would never help me.

"Or perhaps," Mrs. Buttocks says, "some of you are helping each other."

The entire class is silent, not just from not talking but from not moving.

"How many of you work with someone on your math homework?"

No one raises a hand. No one moves a muscle.

"I see," she says, and picks up a stack of papers. "Just as I thought. No one will fess up. So today I'm giving a pop quiz. Surprise! You'll turn in it at the end of class with your homework. It'll be the same sheet as your homework."

The room remains still. Everyone is quiet, but not quiet like the library. And not quiet like my family when we're mad at each other. It's a different kind of quiet. It's like heavy and quiet at the same time.

Mrs. Buttocks moves down the rows, and her clogs clunk on the linoleum floor. *Clunk, clunk, clunk, clunk, clunk.* Her steps are heavy and slow and evenly paced. She shifts her body between the desks and places a quiz on Mimi's desk face down. She gets to my desk and gives me a quiz, face down.

"Good luck," she tells me, not smiling.

I turn the quiz over, and it's exactly as I expect: impossible. It's the same long division homework sheet I struggled with last night. I don't see how doing it a second time will make it any easier.

I write my name and date at the top of the quiz. Now, at least, there's one thing I won't get wrong. Then I line up the long division problem the way I've been taught, and halfway through the problem I'm out of numbers but still haven't finished the borrowing and carrying. So I try to erase the problem, but the pencil mark smears into a big blob instead of disappearing. What a mess. I move to the next problem.

Four. Eight. Division sign. Six. Four. Four. One. Nine.

I don't know how to do that one either.

At the end of class Mrs. Buttocks comes around to collect our papers, and I hand her my quiz and homework. Both are covered in eraser marks and smeared pencil, and I'll be lucky to get one math problem right between the two.

Weird thing is, Mrs. Buttocks smiles at me like I did an amazing job.

"Thank you, Bag," she says.

She grabs Mimi's quiz from her desk.

"And your homework?" Mrs. Buttocks says to Mimi.

"I didn't do it," Mimi says.

Which is weird. Mimi always gets A's on her homework. Mimi always gets everything right.

"Amelia." Mrs. Buttocks shakes her head. "How disappointing."

She holds Mimi's quiz in her hand. I see lots of eraser marks, and Mimi didn't finish the last two problems. What's going on? The bell rings. We're dismissed and I leave feeling like my terrible pop quiz might be the best thing I'll do today. It's a very strange feeling.

In another turn of unusual events, Minerva is waiting in the hallway.

"We need to talk," she says.

I glance over my shoulder, figuring she's saying this to Mimi.

"Now," Minerva says.

"Me?"

"Of course you." My sister pulls me to an empty corner.

"I've got to go," I say. "It's time for lunch."

"You're not going anywhere." Minerva takes my hand, maneuvers me to a bench next to a water fountain, and forces me to sit. She sits next to me and leans in. "Why are you sabotaging Mimi?"

"What?" My mind spins. I push my glasses up the bridge of my nose.

Minerva shakes her head at my glasses. "Is that supposed to be intimidating?"

Not intimidating. Magic. I wish the glasses were magic and gave me the power to peer into the true thoughts in her head, not the phony ones that come out of her mouth.

Minerva says, "Mimi told me you bumped into her on purpose."

"Mimi didn't tell you anything," I say, thrilled to have caught Minerva in a lie. "Mimi and I had math together, like we always do. She didn't mention anything to me."

Minerva looks down the narrow hallway to see if anyone is coming. "Fine," she says. "I saw you. I was waiting for Mimi and I saw you. You pretended to bump into her, and then you guys started talking."

Finally a snippet of truth comes out of my sneaky sister. Her hands are a little bit shaky, and she shoves them under her butt. "So, are you going to tell me what you know? Or are you going to make me beg?"

I would love to see my sister beg, so I keep quiet.

Minerva looks up at the ceiling and groans. "Okay, let's just get down to it. You bribed Mimi. What did she ask for?"

"Bribe Mimi?" I hold that thought in my head and let Minerva dig herself deeper into a story I'm still piecing together.

"Oh," Minerva says. "I get it. You want me to bribe you. Fine. What do you want?"

Random Thought 519.2

Holy smokes, I might get something out of this?

"What do you have to offer?" I ask.

"I'm not the one who sets the bribe, moron. You are."

"I want all of the Popsicles after dinner."

"Done."

"I want to be left alone to read when we're in the house."

"Done."

"And . . . I want you to stop what you're doing."

"How do you know what I'm doing?"

"I want you to stop."

My sister clenches her jaw. "I'm not stopping."

"Minerva," I say, "it's really bad, and it's going to damage the rest of your life."

"What are you talking about?"

"The smoking, Minerva. You're getting cigarettes from Mimi in exchange for doing her math homework."

Minerva shifts uncomfortably on the bench and looks lost, like a salt-and-pepper set that's missing the pepper. The bell rings above us and snaps her back into her confident self. "That's what you think is happening?"

"So you'll stop?" I say.

"Stop what?" she says.

"The smoking."

"You're such an idiot." Minerva stands up. "Smoking is disgusting. I would never touch a cigarette." Then she scurries down the hall.

chapter nineteen

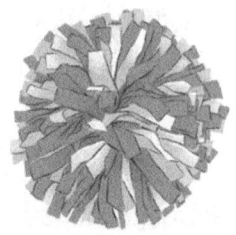

AT MY REGULAR LUNCH TABLE, THE ONE FARTHEST away from the hot-lunch line, I pull out my Lunch by Lenore.

The cafeteria is full of people. I hear the clink of silverware against plastic lunch trays and fast-paced chatter between friends. The sounds don't go together. The room is noisy and out of sync. I wish I could close my ears. I sigh. I'm not hungry and I'm sitting alone and it's embarrassing.

I stare at the double doors of the cafeteria, trying to make Ridgley magically appear and sit next to me. I want to tell him about *The Old Man and the Sea*, the beginning and the end. I want to ask him about Chekhov. I want everything to go back to normal.

My eyes stay locked on the doors, and Mimi walks in without Minerva. Then a gaggle of cheerleaders walk in without Minerva. The boy from my locker mistake walks in.

He's sees me and elbows the girl next to him. She wears a black sweater and black jeans and black eyeliner and black boots. I have a feeling she's Anna Beth, the girl with the PUNK sticker on her locker. They both start to laugh.

I take a deep breath and look at the ceiling. I feel like my dad, last night, when he pulled up in his old Honda with the carpet stains and the cup holder full of coins. I take another deep breath. *Please, Mother Nature, or whoever who might be listening, please tell Ridgley to come sit next to me. Please. I don't want to sit alone.*

When I open my eyes, I don't believe it. My wish came true. It's Ridgley. He's walking through the double doors. He stares at me, and I feel powerful, like my talk with Mother Nature just made him appear.

Ridgley's brown eyes meet mine. He sees me at our regular table.

I hold up my Lunch by Lenore. "Want some?" I mouth.

He looks away from me, heads over to the hot-lunch line, where the menu is beef franks and beans. I can't believe Ridgley is passing up my mom's lunch for a plate of beans. Why won't he sit with me?

He gets his food in the lunch line. Then he takes his tray piled high with glistening brown slop and sits down at the advanced students' table.

My insides start to ache again.

I toss my Lunch by Lenore onto the empty table. There's no way I'm going to eat it. My stomach feels too terrible to put food inside it. The room chatters around me, and I feel the opposite of how I felt yesterday when I was in the cafeteria, and it was empty and clean and good. Now the cafeteria is just noisy and crowded and awful. I figure it can't get any worse.

Not a moment later another Lunch by Lenore swings in front of my face. I look up to see Minerva as she plops herself next to me. "What did you tell Mimi?"

So, turns out I'm wrong. It gets worse.

The cafeteria roars around us. I watch Ridgley take a bite of his beef frank.

"Hello?" Minerva snaps her fingers in front of my face. "Earth to Bag. What did you tell Mimi?"

I take my eyes away from Ridgley. "Nothing."

"It can't be nothing."

"I don't know," I say. "I asked if her parents smoked cigarettes."

"That's it?"

"Yeah."

"What happened in math?"

"We had a quiz. Why?"

My sister pulls out a kebob and unwraps the foil. She shoves a hunk of chicken into her mouth and starts to chew as if she's hungry or nervous or maybe a bit of both.

Before she finishes chewing her colossal bite, she talks with her mouth full. "Mimi's out."

"Out of what?" I ask. "Cigarettes?"

At the word "cigarettes" an eighth-grade boy from the table next to ours raises his eyebrows at my sister.

"Keep your voice down," Minerva whispers, but kids can still hear her. "I need you to meet me after school, before the game. We can talk about it then. Meet me in the gym. I have something to show you."

"Are you smoking cigarettes?" I whisper. I don't want anyone to hear us, but I can't stop myself from asking. I need to know.

"Of course not," Minerva replies.

Our eyes lock, and then she looks away.

I don't know if I believe her. If it's not cigarettes, I'm scared she's doing something worse. Bottom line: I need to know what she's hiding. I need to go to cheerleading.

Minerva inhales the rest of her Lunch by Lenore.

"I'll meet you in the gym," I say.

She looks up from her food. "Thank you," she says. "I mean it. Thank you."

I notice an unusual expression on her face. It's not anger or frustration or impatience, which is usually how she looks at me. It takes me a minute to place it, before I realize: It's gratitude.

chapter twenty

LAST CLASS OF THE DAY AND I'M TIRED. I'M tired of worrying about Minerva and I'm tired because I never ate my lunch and I'm tired because English is going to start any minute and I don't have the energy to think about any of this.

Mr. Perkins looks tired too. He's sitting at his desk, holding a mug of coffee. Steam rises from the top like fog rolling over the ocean. He blows on the coffee and then takes a huge slurp as kids trickle into the room. Today he's wearing a shirt with no words, and his blazer is hanging on a coat hanger on a hook behind his desk. We've got two minutes until the bell rings.

Ridgley's already here. He's sitting at his desk two away from mine, reading the end of *The Seagull*. He never said hi to me. He never looked up when I walked past his desk.

His face stays hidden behind his book, even when I walk over and stand in front of him. I'm a foot away and cross my arms over my chest. He tilts his head down and looks at my sneakers. I know he knows it's me, because I'm the only kid at school who wears maroon slip-on sneakers. I can't hold it in any longer.

"Is it my glasses?" I ask.

"What?" He looks up from *The Seagull*.

"Because I don't need glasses?"

"You don't need glasses?"

"Is that why you're mad?"

"I'd never be mad at you for that."

I take off my glasses and hold them in front of me. "They're not prescription, just plain glass. They're fake."

He says, "I like your glasses."

My hands shake as I put the glasses back onto my face. Everyone's looking at me because now they all know. They know I don't need glasses. It's like I'm in one of those awful dreams. The dream when I'm at school and I don't have clothes on and everyone is laughing.

Except I do have clothes on, and nobody is laughing. Instead the kids in the room stare at me in silence. It's awful, the silence. They know I'm stupid, and I have to stand in front of them holding the quiet truth.

I close my eyes. I wish I were in a nightmare. I wish I were anywhere but here.

With my eyes closed, I'm worried I'm going to cry. I'm worried huge tears are going to leak through the seam where my eyelids meet my skin, trickle off my lashes, and fog up my fake glasses. So I open my eyes and blink back tears.

Then my eyes meet Ridgley's. He's so calm, sitting there looking at me, and I'm furious. I'm furious that he won't tell me what I've done.

"Why are you mad at me?" I ask.

"I'm not mad at you," he says.

The late bell rings above us. I vaguely hear Mr. Perkins telling me to sit down, but I'm not listening. My attention is locked on Ridgley. I keep going. "Of course you're mad at me."

"I'm not."

"You ignored me at lunch."

Ridgley looks down.

I keep my eyes fixed on him. "Just tell me what's going on."

"Margaret." Ridgley looks right at me. "I mean, the cheerleading, and I saw you talking with Sherman earlier today, and—"

"What are you talking about?" I step back from him. "I don't even know who Sherman is."

"The center on the basketball team."

"I thought his name was Sheldon."

Ridgley scuffs his boot against the floor. He doesn't say anything back. Which is the worst. I want him to say something back. Friends tell each other the truth. But he doesn't. He just sits there.

"I thought we were friends," I say.

He looks at me, like he wants to say something.

"It's just that . . . " he says.

"Friends tell each other the truth," I say.

He stops talking. Clearly he doesn't want to be friends.

"Excuse me!"

A voice floods my ears. I hear him before I realize who it is. I remember I'm in English. Mr. Perkins is talking to me. "Bag," he says, "Ridgley. Both of you. Class has started, and I'm not going to ask again. Please, take a seat."

My mind fills faster than a water balloon connected to a running faucet. It gets bigger and bigger, and now Mr. Perkins is mad at me and Ridgley doesn't want to be my friend and I don't know how to make it stop and it's too much and . . .

I open my mouth.

"Why am I even in advanced English? I can barely read."

The class laughs because they think I'm making a joke. Mr. Perkins looks at me with sad eyes and says, "Let's talk after class."

The class laughs louder, and I feel like the biggest jerk. Now I'm like Dad's car abandoned on the side of the road with smoke billowing out from the hood.

"Let's focus, people." Mr. Perkins's voice sounds clipped. "We've got a lot to cover today."

It's too much. I can't take another word. I stumble toward my desk and sit down. My body is here, but my head goes somewhere else.

Random Thought 133.8
I'm in the clouds. I'm in the air. I'm
floating like the thoughts inside my
brain are leaving my body the same way
a butterfly leaves a cocoon.

It isn't until the middle of class when my head returns to my shoulders. Once again I'm in English. I'm sitting in front of Mr. Perkins. He speaks to the class. On the whiteboard he scribbles words: "thoughtful," "curious," "sad," and "angry."

Ridgley won't look at me.

My head feels woozy. My stomach aches and rolls around like a lava lamp. *Please, please, please don't throw up.* Throwing up is the one bad thing that actually hasn't happened to me today.

Mr. Perkins has a book in his hand, *The Wednesday Wars*. He opens it. He stops at the first page of the book.

Then he writes a sentence on the board. It's the first sentence. Wonderful. Why doesn't he write the last sentence? What's the point of knowing the beginning and then reading the whole book if the ending is going to be awful? Please, please. I send my brain waves toward Mr. Perkins. Please erase that sentence and start with the end.

But no. He keeps writing the first sentence. This day just keeps getting worse. The only thing left for him to do is ask me to read the first sentence out loud. Oh god, no. Please, please, please don't make me read out loud.

Mr. Perkins clears his throat and reads the first sentence himself.

"Of all the kids in the seventh grade at Camillo Junior High, there was one kid that Mrs. Baker hated with heat whiter than the sun. Me."

He asks the class, "Does anyone know what the tone of this writing is?"

Ridgley says, "It's funny."

"Yes, but what's underneath the humor?"

"It's pretty," Mimi says. "The way heat can be whiter than the sun."

"It is," Mr. Perkins says. "Anything else?"

"It's alliteration," a kid says from the back of the room. "'Hated' and 'heat.'"

"Good," Mr. Perkins says. "Anything else?"

I think the tone has something to do with an emotion,

but I don't raise my hand. There's no way I want to look like an even bigger fool than I already do. The word "me" repeats in my head. *Me. Me. Me.*

Before I can stop myself I say, "Maybe the tone is lonely."

"Why do you think that?" Mr. Perkins asks.

"Because the 'me.' . . . It's the only word in the sentence."

"Excellent," Mr. Perkins says. "I think the tone is lonely too."

I can't help myself. This day has been the absolute worst, but my mouth cracks into a tiny smile. Maybe I'm bad at most things, but I sure am able to spot loneliness when I need to.

Random Thought 823
The Wednesday Wars sounds like a really good book.

At the end of class I'm still thinking about the sentence.

The bell rings above me.

"Bag," Mr. Perkins calls out, "I'd like to see you, please."

Oh no. I forgot. I forgot about the stupid thing I said. *That I can barely read.* Oh no, oh no, oh no. I don't want Mr. Perkins to be disappointed with me.

I grab my bag, stand up, and stumble toward his desk. My hands are shaky and I'm super embarrassed to talk to him.

"Everything okay?" Mr. Perkins says.

"I guess."

He rests his elbows on his desk and leans toward me. "You belong in this class, Bag."

"Not really."

"Why would you say that?"

"Because . . ." I don't want to say I'm dyslexic. I'm sure he knows. I'm sure there's some file about me in the principal's office that explains my problem.

Mr. Perkins glances at the stack of books on his desk. *The Wednesday Wars* is on top. "Reading is more than stringing together letters and words." He picks up the book. "Reading takes understanding. Reading takes empathy. You have that in spades."

"Thanks, Mr. Perkins."

He hands me *The Wednesday Wars*. "In case you want to finish it."

I take the book into my hands and say, "I do."

chapter twenty-one

I STEP INTO THE HALLWAY AND IT'S EMPTY. I thought my talk with Mr. Perkins was quick, but it must've taken longer than I realized. It looks like school ended thirty minutes ago, rather than five. Weird.

I hoped Ridgley might be waiting for me in the hallway. To talk about what happened in Mr. Perkins's class. I'm not exactly sure what just happened in Mr. Perkins's class. But Ridgley isn't in the hallway. Nobody is. Which makes my stomach hurt and feel hollow at the same time.

I stand in the hallway, feeling awful. I don't know what to do with myself, so I open my backpack, and there it is. *The Wednesday Wars*. I take the book out of my backpack and sigh. The brand-new jacket feels cool and slick in my hands.

Hold on. Earth to Bag. I'm supposed to meet Minerva.

Get it together, Bag!

I shove the book into my pack and speed toward the gym. The school stays quiet. I don't see teachers or kids. A faint humming sound grows louder with each one of my steps. It's super weird. But I keep going.

I rush past the little bench where Minerva pushed me to sit. I pass the locker with the PUNK sticker. I pass the cafeteria, and the teachers' lounge. The closer I get to the gym, the louder the hum, until it turns into chatter, stomping, shuffling, basketballs hitting against the gym floor.

Basketballs? Hold on. It's not just cheerleading practice today. There's a basketball game. A playoff game. The halls are empty because everyone is at the gym. Everyone except me.

I round the corner and bump directly into Mrs. Yoh.

"Bag?"

Mrs. Yoh's face is inches from my own. We're so close that our noses are almost touching.

"It's game day," she says. "And not just any game. It's the playoffs! We're going to need help with the uniforms."

She ushers me through the crowded gym, then pulls the storage closet door open. The room is filled with girls but empty of sound. The cheerleaders are all sitting cross-legged with their hands resting palms up on top of their thighs. Their eyes are closed.

"We're having five minutes of silent meditation," Mrs. Yoh whispers. "To gather and collect our energy for the game. The power of positive thinking is astounding. I read about it on the internet."

The girls are already wearing their uniforms, and their hair has been brushed into perfect ponytails. My eyes find Minerva. Her eyes are closed, but I notice that her mouth moves the tiniest bit as she gnaws on her bottom lip.

Mrs. Yoh sighs deeply. Then she claps her hands together. "Alrighty! That's a wrap on the meditation. Wonderful, girls. Just wonderful!" She turns to me. "Now, Bag. Can you help with these patches?" She grabs a pile of fuzzy patch stickers. "For our all-stars!" Mrs. Yoh says. "Every sticker has a personalized initial. Make sure each girl gets the correct one."

The cheerleaders stand and start to get in line formation.

"Stay focused, now," Mrs. Yoh tells them. "We've got a game to win." She hands me the patches.

"Minerva," Mrs. Yoh says. "Let's practice the opening cheer. We can run that first."

Minerva glances at me. "I'm still writing it, Mrs. Yoh."

"Still writing it? Oh my word." Mrs. Yoh looks woozy, and she runs her hands through her feathered bangs. "How are you not done? The game is in fifteen minutes!"

"I'm almost done, but I want to get the ending right."

"Well, it's a very important cheer. It sets the tone for the entire game. The players are counting on us. They need our presence and focus. We can't let them down! We can't let ourselves down!" Mrs. Yoh shakes her head and closes her eyes like she's thinking really hard. "Okay," she finally says. "Why don't you take five minutes to work on it quietly outside the room?"

"Sure, Mrs. Yoh." Minerva scoots toward the door, past Mimi.

Mimi won't look at Minerva.

"Mimi?" Mrs. Yoh says. "Are you going to take notes?"

Minerva says, "Bag can do it."

"Bag?" Mrs. Yoh says my name like she's completely forgotten who I am. Then she looks at me. "Of course! Bag!" Not a moment later Mrs. Yoh takes the patches out of my hands and gives them to Mimi. "Make sure each girl gets her very own personalized patch."

Mimi takes the patches. Then she narrows her eyes at me.

At the same time, Minerva makes a coughing sound to get my attention. My eyes meet hers and we hurry out of the room together. Back in the closet we hear Mrs. Yoh shout, "Girls! Let's run cheer number two! Places, everyone!"

Minerva sprints to the cafeteria, and I follow. She's fast, and it's hard to keep up, but I will my legs to stay in rhythm with hers. One and two and one and two . . .

My sneakers hit the linoleum floor like sticks on a drum. I'm running as if I hear music. One and two and one and two . . .

Minerva reaches the cafeteria and pushes through the swinging doors, still moving at full speed. I follow behind, keeping time with every one of her footfalls. One and two and . . .

I love the sound of our footsteps.

I barely pay attention to the cafeteria. I notice it's clean, but I'm moving fast and I have so much inside my head. I trail Minerva through the side door that opens to the alley and pray there aren't any rats.

Minerva crouches next to a dumpster. I squat next to her, and she looks at me. Her eyes are as big as half-dollars. She doesn't blink. I have no idea what she's thinking. It's the longest Minerva has ever looked at me without looking away.

"Where were you?" she finally says. "After school."

"Oh," I say. "With my teacher. He wanted to talk about a book." What I don't mention is that he also wanted to talk about why I feel dumb. I also don't mention what happened with Ridgley.

She keeps staring at me. "I waited for you."

"Minerva." I look at my sister crouched beside a smelly dumpster. "What's going on? You can tell me."

She opens her backpack. I feel nervous. I'm certain

she's about to pull out a pack of cigarettes. But . . .

She pulls out a manila folder. It looks like the folder Mimi was carrying this morning. Minerva opens the folder, and I see the math homework Mrs. Buttocks assigned yesterday. It's the homework we had to turn in with our pop quiz. Why does my sister have it?

My head is trying to piece together the information while I stare at the homework. It's written in my sister's handwriting. I can tell by the fours. She makes them look like little flags. The other thing I notice is that the sheet is a copy.

Minerva picks up the top sheet, and there's another exactly like it underneath. I see math homework, I see fours in the shape of flags, and I see that the place to write your name has been left blank.

My head grows dizzy.

Random Thought 571
The body knows before the mind when
something is wrong. That's because
the mind has a funny way of rewriting
the story, but the body can't do that. The
body reacts in a clear, direct way. The
body always tells the truth.

chapter twenty-two

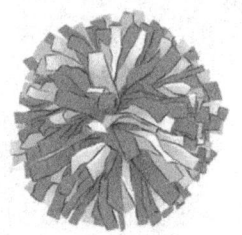

MINERVA PULLS A BOX OF MATCHES FROM a small pouch inside her backpack. She lights a single sheet of homework on fire and drops the paper to the ground. We watch the flames dance and swirl higher and higher next to the dumpster until they get smaller and smaller and fizzle out in a stream of smoke. The smoky air makes me cough and gasp, and I fan my hand in front of my face, trying to clear the smoke away.

"Yuck," I say. "Why are you doing that? It smells awful."

She holds up another sheet of math homework. "The number one rule is, there can't be a trace."

"A trace of what?"

She lights an identical sheet of homework on fire,

and an answer returns to me all at once. "Oh. You're doing Mimi's homework for her?"

"Guess again," she says as the paper's flames grow. The light from the flame flickers against her skin.

"Mimi isn't paying you?" I ask.

Minerva shakes her head. "Mimi was my partner. Five bucks a sheet, and I gave her a dollar for every sale."

"Wait a minute. You mean you're doing homework for someone else in Mrs. Buttocks's class?"

"Try the plural version."

"How many people?"

"Everyone."

Minerva picks up another sheet and lights it on fire. It feels like she's lighting me on fire. The word burns my ears and simmers inside my belly. *Everyone.* She's doing homework for *everyone* in my math class, *everyone*. Except me.

Which is wrong on so many levels. First, she's a cheater and she could totally get expelled from school. Second, I'm terrible at math, and if there's one person who needs help, it's me. But here she is, helping *everyone* else.

Minerva stares at the burning paper. "Mimi gives me that night's homework sheet at practice. I make a copy in the teacher's lounge and complete it while Mimi writes a new cheer. Then I make copies of the finished homework and Mimi gives me her cheer, and while I'm giving the new cheer to Mrs. Yoh, Mimi slips the homework into lockers."

"But the handwriting. The handwriting is the same on all the homework. Why hasn't Mrs. Buttocks figured it out?"

"Nobody turns in the sheet Mimi gives them. They fill out their own sheet with their own handwriting, and they're required to get at least one problem wrong. Mimi does the same thing with her homework and she also gets at least one answer wrong. I burn the original, give Mimi her cut, and we start again."

"Five dollars a sheet? For everyone in Mrs. Buttocks's class?" I try to do the math in my head, but I don't know the exact amount. So I say, "That's a lot of money."

Minerva's eyes dance as if fire has found its way inside them.

"Sure is," she says.

"How much?"

She rubs her hands together. "As of today, nine hundred and sixty-five dollars, minus the one hundred and ninety-three I've given Mimi."

I freeze. My body won't move. My head stops thinking. The only thing I have running through me is fear. "Minerva," I whisper, "this is serious stuff. You could get in so much trouble."

"Stop being dramatic."

She takes the rest of her originals and lights them on fire in one big stack.

"Why do you need that much money?" I ask.

Minerva watches the enormous stack of paper blow up in a tall wall of fire. "How would you like to be my new partner?"

"Hold on," I say.

"You can have a dollar a page. Mimi doesn't want to do it anymore, and I need someone in Mrs. Buttocks's class to pass out the homework and collect the money."

I picture Mrs. Buttocks. I picture our math class from earlier today. I remember her saying that the homework and quizzes weren't lining up.

"Minerva," I say. "Mrs. Buttocks knows."

Minerva's eyes stop dancing. She stares at me. "There's no way she knows."

"She does. She was asking us questions about our homework and how the class gets the homework right but bombs the tests, and then she gave us a pop quiz, and it was the same as the homework."

"Oh my god."

"You have to stop."

"No."

"Minerva, why do you think Mimi quit?"

"Mimi's a coward."

"Mimi knows Buttocks knows."

"Are you in or out?" she asks.

"Minerva, you have to stop."

"I'm almost at my one-thousand-dollar goal."

"Your goal? Why do you need that much money?"

Minerva stands up. "You're either in or out."

I don't know what to do. She's totally going to get caught. If I help her, I'll get in trouble. If I don't help her, I'll feel like a terrible person, a terrible sister.

"Bag?" A woman's voice calls from the cafeteria. "Minerva? Are you in here?"

Oh no. Oh no. Oh no. What if she opens the side door and sees us in front of the dumpster, in front of this burning paper? She's going to want answers. Oh no. Oh no. Oh no. I don't want to lie to Mrs. Yoh. I don't even know the kind of lie to tell that would get us out of this mess.

Heels click on the linoleum floor. I watch the side door. So does Minerva. My heart races in my chest. I swallow. My heart keeps racing. The side door does not open. Heels click out of the cafeteria.

I sigh, placing my hand over my racing heart.

I look over at my sister.

"You have to stop, Minerva."

She shakes her head.

I continue. "Mrs. Yoh knows you aren't writing cheers in the cafeteria. Mrs. Buttocks knows someone is doing the homework. She gave us a quiz that was exactly like your homework sheet. I'm telling you, she knows. She's going to look for the new sheet tomorrow. If she finds it and she talks to the principal and word gets back to Mrs. Yoh, they're totally going to piece it together. You've got to destroy the new sheet."

Minerva shakes her head again.

"Please," I say. "I don't want you to get in trouble. If you don't destroy the sheets you will get in so much trouble."

My sister bites her bottom lip hard so hard, I'm worried she's going to draw blood. "I can't."

"Yes, you can!"

"No, I can't. I got the sheet from Mimi after school and filled it out at the beginning of cheerleading. By the way, where were you? It took you so long to get here. I already gave the sheet back to Mimi. She said this was her last round and then she's done."

I stand up from where I was crouching. "We have to get it back from her! Before she makes copies and passes them out!"

"Oh my god, the game starts in a few minutes. What if Mrs. Buttocks is there? At the game?" My sister's face has gone as white as a homework sheet before she lights the thing on fire.

"We have to stop her," I say.

Without another word we open the side door and sprint through the cafeteria. There's no need to discuss where we're going.

chapter twenty-three

WE BURST INTO THE STORAGE CLOSET, AND I SEE Mrs. Yoh first. She's holding a clipboard and looks flustered, her normally smooth hair winging out in different directions.

Minerva, wearing her uniform, stands by my side. We hear the crowd in the gym. The game hasn't started, but the excitement surrounds us. People talk, feet smack against the bleachers and basketballs pound against the court as the two teams warm up for the game.

Minerva rushes over to Mimi. I watch Minerva whisper into Mimi's ear. Mimi's mouth turns down with worry. Her face turns grayish white. Mimi whispers something back to Minerva, and Minerva nods. Mimi's frown deepens.

Not a moment later Mrs. Yoh sees Minerva talking to Mimi.

"Minerva!" she says. "Where is that new cheer?"

At the same time, Mimi says in a tiny voice, "Mrs. Yoh?"

"Oh, Mimi," Mrs. Yoh replies. "You don't look well, dear."

"I don't feel well," Mimi says.

"Well, go and lie down. I'm sure the nurse is still in her office. It is a playoff game, after all."

Minerva nods at Mimi. Mimi moves toward the door.

"Wait!" Mrs. Yoh is waving the clipboard in front of her face. "Mimi, you are the top of our pyramid. What on earth are we going to do?"

Mimi pauses near the door.

Mimi, I want to yell. *Go get the homework!* But I can't say that. Think. Think. Think. My eyes find Minerva. Her eyes are staring at me, wide open and afraid.

Before I have time to stop myself, I turn to Mrs. Yoh and say, "I can do it, Mrs. Yoh. I can be the top of the pyramid."

"Oh, Bag, that would be marvelous. Are you sure you're comfortable with this?"

I nod, even though I'm not.

"Well, let's get you a uniform, then. I've got an extra one right over here."

Mrs. Yoh goes over to the corner of the room and rummages through some equipment. Mimi scoots out of the storage closet, and while Mrs. Yoh's back is turned, Minerva follows her.

Mrs. Yoh waves a uniform in the air. Then she rushes over to me. "Here you go, Bag!" She motions to the other cheerleaders that we should head to the gym. "Wait," she says. "What happened to Minerva?"

"She took Mimi to the nurse," I say quickly. "To make sure she's okay."

"Well, where is that new cheer?" Mrs. Yoh says. "Girls, we must start with a new cheer."

"Um," I stumble. "Minerva told me what the new cheer is."

Mrs. Yoh leans toward me. The cheerleaders lean toward me. Our cheerleading circle buzzes with excitement.

Of course there is no new cheer, so I need to make one up on the spot.

"Well . . ." I stall for an idea.

The cheerleaders stare at me. Mrs. Yoh stares at me. I clutch the cheerleading uniform in my hand.

I have absolutely no idea what to say. I don't know anything about cheerleading. I don't know anything about writing cheers. My mind goes blank, and I can't make sense of a single thing. *Please, please, please. Think of an idea. Think!*

The cheerleaders keep looking at me, so I close my eyes. With my eyes closed, I hear noises from the gym. I hear feet on the bleachers. I hear sneakers pounding on the basketball floor. . . .

And just like that, an idea floats toward me. I have no idea if it's a good idea or a bad idea, but at this point I'm out of options. So I say, "You guys remember that clap, clap, stomp thing?"

"Sure," Emily S. says.

"We're going to do that. But don't say the words. We don't need them. We're going to clap, clap, stomp, and clap, clap, stomp together, and we'll get faster and faster. Make sure you're listening and then wait for my cue. When the claps and stomps are superfast, I'll yell 'GO,' and that's when we'll give it to them."

"Give them what?" Emily C. asks.

"We're going to dance."

The cheerleaders hop up and down.

"Dance anyway you want," I say. "Dance the way the basketball players feel when they're playing, when they're excited and nervous and happy. Dance like crazy. Dance the way you dance at home in the mirror."

All the girls stick their hands into the middle of the circle.

"Awesome," Emily C. says.

"Go, team!" everyone shouts.

"Bag, that's fantastic. We'll start with our new cheer."

Mrs. Yoh begins to line the cheerleaders up near the door. Then she turns to me. "Get that uniform on and meet us in the gym. "Quickety quick!" she adds. "The game is about to begin!"

chapter twenty-four

I HAVE NO IDEA WHAT I'M DOING. HOW DID I get myself into this mess? I step onto the sidelines with the cheerleaders. I'm wearing a cheerleading uniform. The only good thing about the uniform is that it's blue, my favorite color.

Everything else is terrible.

The polyester fabric is scratchy against my skin. The collar is tight around my neck. The skirt is way too short. I shift in my sneakers, wishing I was wearing something else. I'd give anything for an ironic T-shirt right now.

The audience waits for us to begin. Oh, dear god, I've got to perform a cheer wearing this completely embarrassing uniform. I can barely remember what I told the cheerleaders. I pull at the hem of my skirt, wishing it were longer. Then I lean over to Emily C. "How does the beginning go?"

"Clap, clap, stomp," she whispers back.

"That's it!" I say.

I start off soft and slow. I feel so nervous that I want to faint. Everyone is watching us from the audience. I see Mrs. Buttocks, Mr. Perkins, Cody or Brody or whatever his name is, Anna Beth . . . and then I see him.

Ridgley.

He's high up in the corner of the bleachers. He's looking at me. He sits in the fourth row from the top, and when he sees me in the cheerleading uniform, he leans forward and places his chin in his hand.

Oh no! I told him I wasn't a cheerleader! Now I'm wearing a cheerleading uniform and I'm about to *cheer*. This is the worst. I told him the truth and, when I said it, I wasn't a cheerleader. Now it looks like I was lying!

My whole body slumps forward. I'm embarrassed by the uniform, so I look away from Ridgley and focus on the beat of the cheer until it becomes the only thing in my mind.

Clap, clap, stomp.

I clap my hands together. I stomp my foot into the floor. I forget about my itchy uniform. I forget about the audience. I make everything about the clapping and the stomping.

Clap, clap, stomp. Clap, clap, stomp.

The cheerleaders join me, and we get faster and

louder and faster and louder. The cheerleaders and me, we're in perfect sync.

Clap, clap, stomp. Clap, clap, stomp. Clap, clap, stomp. Clap, clap, stomp.

Finally, when we can't get any faster or louder, I yell, "Go!"

I close my eyes and pretend I'm dancing in my room with a beat in my head and my bedroom door closed. I pretend I'm alone as I shimmy my hips in circles and wiggle my shoulders in quick little bursts.

I open my eyes and see that the cheerleaders have joined me in my dance. They are doing the dance I do alone. They shimmy their hips and wiggle their shoulders. We are dancing together.

The audience cheers for us. Faces in the audience smile and cheer. Hands clap. I turn to the cheerleaders. They keep dancing and smiling and clapping and waving to the audience. So I do the same. I keep dancing. Then I smile. I clap. I wave to the audience. The cheers grow louder. It feels great!

BWAHHHH!

The game buzzer sounds, and the playoff game has begun.

The cheerleaders hug me and steer me toward the bleachers like we're a flock of birds. I take a seat on the floor in front of the bleachers. Mrs. Yoh leans over and squeezes my shoulder.

"Amazing," she whispers.

Mrs. Yoh sits behind us. The cheerleaders gather around me. I'm in the center of them, and my heart is pounding faster than a rocket ship. I'm so excited.

Then I see Minerva.

I forgot about her.

She's standing at the side of the gym. And she's crying.

chapter twenty-five

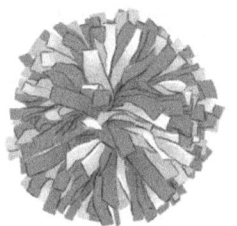

"MINERVA!" MRS. YOH SHOUTS. "OVER HERE, DEAR!"

I turn around. Mrs. Yoh is waving at my sister. I turn back to face Minerva. She's still standing at the side of the gym, opposite from where we sit in front of the bleachers. I mouth the words, "Are you okay?"

Minerva glares at me. She isn't crying anymore. Her eyes narrow into little slits. She looks at Mrs. Yoh and smiles. Her smile is wide and friendly. Minerva goes from crying to glaring to smiling in less than one second. It's bizarre. Was she even crying? Not a moment later, Minerva rushes over and shoves herself next to me and the other cheerleaders.

"Where's Mimi?" I ask.

Minerva doesn't respond.

From behind us Mrs. Yoh places her hand on my

shoulder. "Bag had an amazing first cheer!" she tells my sister. Then she gives me another little squeeze, removes her hand from my shoulder, and goes back to watching the game.

I lean closer to Minerva and whisper, "Did you find her? Did Mimi get the homework back?"

Again Minerva doesn't respond.

At the same time, Mrs. Yoh pats my head again. "That little stomp, stomp part was wonderful! What a natural dancer you are, Bag!"

Embarrassed to have so much attention, I turn to face her and shrug. "Thanks, Mrs. Yoh. I'm glad you liked it."

Mrs. Yoh places her hand on her heart. "I loved it."

I turn back around and look at my sister. She rolls her eyes.

"Are you okay?" I ask.

"No," Minerva says. "I'm not. I saw your little cheer."

A ball swishes into the basket. The crowd explodes. We turn and face the game. The scoreboard says two more points for us. The crowd claps and we cheer, "Two points! Two points! Two points! Yay!"

Then, out of nowhere, I feel a jab in my side. Minerva elbowed me. Then she pinches my arm. "Ouch!" I hold my side. "Why did you do that?"

The buzzer sounds again, and the boys rush off the court.

"Let's do the time-out cheer!" Mrs. Yoh says.

The cheerleaders hop up. Minerva hops up herself and follows the other cheerleaders onto the court. She puts on her happy face and runs to her spot, the spot that is front and center.

Of course, I don't know what the time-out cheer is, and my body hurts where my sister just elbowed and pinched me. I don't like my uniform. The only reason I'm here is to help Minerva. I have no idea why she's being mean to me.

"Bag!" Mrs. Yoh says from behind me. "Go! Join them!"

I sigh, knowing there's no way out of this. Before I know it, I'm on the court next to my sister, and I'm so caught up watching Minerva that I forget I'm supposed to be cheering, until I hear, "Sock it to them, sock it to them, hit 'em where it hurts!" The girls say the line over and over. "Sock it to them, sock it to them, hit 'em where it hurts."

I refuse to say those words. Not only are they unsportsmanlike—"hit" is a very aggressive-sounding word—but the cheer is also grammatically incorrect. "'Em" is not in the dictionary. So instead of cheering, I become a mime. The cheerleaders cheer, and I act like I'm acting out what they're saying.

"Hit," they say.

I hold my hand out.

"'Em," they say.

I push my hands as if I'm pushing into someone.

"Where."

I kick my foot out.

"It."

I kick my other foot out.

"Hurts!"

The crowd looks back at me. I see confused faces, wrinkled foreheads. No one is cheering. My body grows hot, and I look at the other cheerleaders. They ignore me as they continue to cheer. I want to dunk my head into a snowbank. I should've never done the mime. I want to be anywhere other than here.

Then Minerva comes over and stands in front of me. "Go with it," she whispers. Then she falls flat onto her face. Her body is sprawled across the gym floor. She dramatically keeps her hands spread across the floor with her body face down.

I kick my foot in the air.

Minerva rolls to her side.

"Hit 'em where it hurts!" the cheerleaders say.

Minerva rolls to her other side.

Now the crowd is laughing. Mrs. Yoh is laughing. Minerva pops up from the floor as the cheerleaders finish the cheer.

"Stomp them to the ground!" Minerva and the cheerleaders say.

Then they all hold their arms up in the air.

The crowd explodes into applause.

The cheerleaders circle around me.

"Great cheer!"

"That was funny, Bag!"

"Super funny!"

I don't know who says what. They all talk over each other and tap their hands against me.

A whistle blows, and we run off the court. The basketball players run back on. I crouch next to Minerva on the floor.

"Thanks," I say. "You saved me back there."

"You are so annoying," Minerva replies.

The little bubble of happiness I felt at being on the same team as Minerva bursts. "What's your problem? You helped me with the cheer. I had no idea what I was doing. I'm thanking you!"

"I didn't want to help you. I did it for the team."

She might be saying that, but I know she didn't have to help me. She wanted to help me. Now I want to help her.

"Did you get the homework?" I ask. "Where's Mimi?"

"She already put the homework into the lockers."

"Wait. What? That's awful. She has to get the homework back."

"She can't."

Swish! Our team scores a three-pointer. Everyone is yelling. The cheerleaders chant, "Three points! Three points! Three points! Yay!" and Mrs. Yoh whoops and hollers like a maniac.

Minerva leans over and pinches me again.

"Ouch!" I rub the spot on my arm. "What is your problem?"

"YOU."

"What are you talking about?"

"YOU ARE MY STUPID PROBLEM!"

"Are you kidding? I'm here to help you."

"You did it on purpose," she hisses. "With the cheer. The dancing. Being funny. You're always trying to get attention by being pathetic. With Mom and your stupid trips to the library. With Dad and your stupid car rides. And now you're doing it here. With cheerleading. It's so annoying. You're the worst."

"What are you talking about? I'm here to help you. I thought we were helping each other!"

"Help me?" She shakes her head. "I don't need any help."

My throat feels tight and dry. I don't know how to respond. "I don't even like cheerleading!" I finally say. "I'm here because I'm worried about YOU."

"Girls," Mrs. Yoh says behind us. "Attention on the game!"

I'm fuming. I can't believe my sister.

The rest of the game passes like a movie I'm barely watching. Maybe Mrs. Yoh can tell I'm out of it. She never calls for the pyramid. I never have to get on top. I stay pressed next to Minerva, who continues to ignore me. Our team scores a ton of baskets. Before I know it, the buzzer sounds. Our team won. The gym erupts in applause. The cheerleaders hop up and start cheering.

Mrs. Yoh shouts, "We're in the finals!"

The crowd is now on their feet. I turn to my sister. We're still sitting on the floor in front of the bleachers. "Minerva," I say in a serious voice. "I want to help you, not hurt you. I'm telling you the truth about Mrs. Buttocks. She knows. I promise. Mimi has to get the homework back."

"The finals are tomorrow." Minerva balls her hands into fists. "You'd better not be here."

chapter twenty-six

AS IF THINGS COULDN'T GET ANY WORSE, MOM'S LATE.

Minerva and I are back on the bench. We're sitting outside the gym. It's cold. I rub my hands together and blow into them. Then I shove my hands into the pockets of my wool coat. I'm still wearing the cheerleading uniform underneath, but I wish I was wearing something warmer. I don't think I've ever been this cold before.

Minerva won't look at me. She won't speak to me. She hasn't said a word since she told me she didn't want me at the game tomorrow. She's wearing her white puffer coat with the same cheerleading uniform underneath. Her hands are also shoved into her pockets. She stares at the empty road in front of us.

Neither one of us mentions that Mom's late.

Inside the gym Mrs. Yoh was chatting with the

basketball coach. Mrs. Yoh doesn't know we're out here, doesn't know Mom is late again. The gym doors swing open. I'm expecting to see Mrs. Yoh. I figure, like last time, she'll pull her car around and wait with us.

But it's not Mrs. Yoh walking through the door.

It's the center on the basketball team. Why did Ridgley bring him up today? What's the player's name again? Sheldon? Now Sheldon is leaving the gym. He's got a jacket over his uniform. He's walking with his parents. They stand on either side of him.

"You were great out there," his dad says.

"I love watching you play," his mom says.

I can't remember when my family ever walked like that, me and Minerva in the middle, Mom and Dad on the outside. If it happened, it was in New York. Dad was probably next to me, Mom next to Minerva. I'm certain we have never walked like that in Rhode Island.

The mom squeezes Sheldon's arm. I watch them. He doesn't look at me. Instead he gives Minerva a quick glance. She shakes her head, then quickly looks to the ground. The basketball player and his parents head to the parking lot.

"What was that about?" I ask.

Minerva ignores me.

"Sheldon gave you a look."

"No, he didn't.

"Why did Sheldon give you a look?"

"He didn't. And his name is Sherman."

"Is it about the homework?"

She goes back to ignoring me.

I pull out *The Old Man and the Sea*. "Fine. Be that way. Don't tell me. I'm done trying to help you." I open to the middle of the book. My brain tries to make sense of the words, but my hands are freezing cold holding the page. Thoughts keep swirling around in my head. My eyes land on the line "This will kill him, the old man thought. He can't do this forever." I think the old man is talking about the fish. Or himself.

"Oh please," Minerva says.

I look up from the book.

Her eyes are in little slits, her lips pinched together. She looks ready to blow. "You tried to steal my spot as head cheerleader!" she says.

"What? No, I didn't."

"And now!" Her voice is loud. "You're, like, super sneaky and back to being a bookworm. When all you really want is to be head cheerleader. It's all or nothing with you. I saw your little dance. You got the cheerleaders to dance with you. Mrs. Yoh said it was amazing. You want to be head cheerleader. You only pretended to help me with the homework."

"That's ridiculous," I say. "Who would ever make me head cheerleader? I'm no good at being a *regular* cheerleader."

The phrase sticks in my throat. *No good.* My throat aches. *No good. No good. No good.* The aching won't go away.

She looks right at me. "You only think about yourself. You never think about me. You should've never joined cheerleading."

I ball my hands into fists. I'm tired of her getting everything wrong. I say, "If it's anyone's fault, it's yours, not mine. I didn't even want to go to cheerleading. I did it for you!"

"Yeah, right. You don't care about me. All you care about is yourself and books. Books. Books. Books." She flings her hand into the air as if she were tossing out a bag of trash. "You'd totally trade me in for a big old stack of books."

"That's not all I care about." My voice quivers. "It's just that, I need to focus on reading because . . ." I take a breath. "Reading helps me. Reading helps me feel not so dumb."

"Then why do you read such stupid things?" She motions toward the book in my hand. "I mean, what are you reading now? *The Old Guy on a Boat?*"

"The Old Man and the Sea."

She looks at me like she's going to laugh. I press my lips together. I don't want her to laugh at my book. I don't want her to laugh at me. I never talk about my reading, never talk about my dyslexia, never talk about how hard it is for me. There's no way I want her to know any of this.

"Why would anyone want to read about an old man?" she asks.

I say, "I like the old man. He's trying to catch a big fish and he's on a tiny boat, and he's having a hard time. . . ."

My throat aches as if I just got elbowed in the windpipe.

"The old man sounds like a huge downer," Minerva says.

My throat aches and tightens, aches and tightens.

Minerva keeps going.

"I mean, if you're going to read a book, why not choose a good one?" Minerva shoves her hands back into her pockets. "Like a book about a character who falls in love. Or wins the lottery. Or does something super exciting."

I hold the book toward my chest. She doesn't understand the old man at all. And I don't understand her. "Dad loves this book."

Minerva groans. "Enough about Dad and what he loves. I mean, didn't you see him yesterday? In the driveway?"

"Yeah, I'm the one who went to get ice cream with him."

"Bag, he had on his sunglasses."

"He always wears his sunglasses."

"It was nighttime. Do you really think he needed sunglasses?"

"Then why would he wear them?"

"He was high."

The word lingers around me like poison. I don't want to breathe. I don't want to take it in. I shift my body on the bench. "No, he wasn't."

"Okay, fine. He always wears his sunglasses. You think he's the greatest, and I'm just some mean, cranky, horrible person who hates him."

Minerva is mean and cranky and horrible sometimes, but I can't stop my throat from aching, my stomach from dropping. "He's getting better," I say. "Mom's just waiting for him to get completely better before he comes back."

"Sure. That must be the plan. What do I know?"

"He's doing the steps," I tell her. "He sits in circles with his friends."

"Uh-huh." Minerva looks up at the starless sky. "Whatever you say."

"He's got a patch," I say. "On his arm. It's for cigarettes. It's the last thing he's got to kick."

"Patches are for other things too."

"Dad said cigarettes."

"Oh sure, okay, I'm certain he's telling the truth." Minerva shakes her head like she's certain he's lying.

"Why are you so hard on him?" I ask.

She doesn't respond.

It's like Dad says, *She's got fire in her blood.*

But then I see her hands. Her fingers tremble. I realize that maybe she isn't being mean. Maybe, just maybe, she's actually worried about him.

The frosty air hangs heavy between us. My throat keeps aching. It hurts so much, I'm not able to swallow. I stare at the book in my hands. The cover has a picture of a man on a boat. I can't look away. It hits me all at once.

"Minerva," I mumble. "What if Dad's like the man from *The Old Man and the Sea*? What if he lives in a tiny place? What if he doesn't like it?"

She doesn't respond.

I remember the other library books I've read.

The Catcher in the Rye. A kid named Holden, misunderstood by his teachers, his friends, his family.

Ask the Dust. A writer named Arturo and nobody likes his writing and he falls in love with a waitress and he can't find her at the end and he throws away his writing and ends up alone.

I clutch *The Old Man and the Sea* toward my chest.

What if I'm picking books that are like my dad? What if I'm picking books that are like me? What if I end up alone too?

My throat aches and tightens again, aches and tightens. The phrase "no good" is back in my throat. *No good. No good. No good.*

Random Thought 126

I'm just no good. I'm no good at reading. I'm no good at cheerleading. I'm no good at math. I'm no good at knowing my right from my left. I'm no good at concentrating. I'm no good at helping Minerva. I'm no good at helping my dad. What if he's no good? What if we're both no good? What if that's the thing I inherited from him? Being no good at everything.

I'm thinking so much, and my hands are so cold, that *The Old Man and the Sea* slips from my grasp. The book falls to the ground. I bend over to pick it up, and my hands are trembling. My whole body is trembling.

Then I feel a hand on my shoulder.

"Bag," Minerva says.

Her hand reaches down and holds mine. Her fingers feel foreign, like I'm holding a clump of Silly Putty. It's the first time we've held hands since we were little. Even though it feels strange, I don't want to let go.

"It's going to be okay," she says.

I'm not exactly sure what she means, but her words are comforting, like a warm blanket being wrapped around me.

We stay like that, holding hands, waiting for Mom. Even though we don't talk about Dad, or Mom, or cheerleading, or homework, it feels like she understands. It feels like maybe, at least to Minerva, at least in this small moment, I'm just a little bit good.

chapter twenty-seven

I WANT OUT OF THE TRUCK.

Mom showed up twenty-five minutes late. She never said sorry. She never asked about the basketball game. She never noticed that Minerva and I were holding hands. She never wanted to know why. All she wants to do is talk about the play.

"The first full run-through couldn't have gone better!" she says.

Minerva and I don't respond.

Mom's wearing her costume from the play. She's got on stained clothing with rips in the knees and an oversized sweater. Her hair is tangled. Part of a garbage bag has been taped to her shoulder. Her costume might look like a homeless person, but her face doesn't look homeless at all. Her face looks really happy. She smiles an enormous grin, like it's no big deal she showed up twenty-five minutes late and we were waiting outside in the freezing cold.

The truck is quiet. I'm stuck in the middle seat. The heat is cranked up so high, I have to wriggle out of my wool jacket. I take it off and shove it under my butt. Now I'm just wearing the itchy polyester cheerleading uniform. My armpits are sweating. It's the worst car ride, with the exception that Minerva isn't being mean to me. She hasn't said a single mean thing since she held my hand.

Mom fills the truck with more of her words. The trash bag crinkles against the seat. "Girls!" she exclaims. "What a treat! Both of you in uniforms!"

Neither one of us replies.

Mom keeps going. "Baggie, you look wonderful as a cheerleader!"

I don't respond to her comment about the way I look. Instead I say, "Your homeless costume is very believable."

"Thanks!" she says. "The run-through was amazing! In fact, our director wants to have a run-through for family and friends tomorrow afternoon, just to see how the lines are landing. I'd love if you girls could come."

"Can't," Minerva says. "Championship game is tomorrow."

"Oh, that's right!" Mom says. "Good for you, Minerva."

"Bag can go to your run-through for family and friends," Minerva replies. "I don't want her at cheerleading."

"What?" I mumble. "Are you kidding?"

"Not kidding," she says.

What happened to our nice moment on the bench? Why is Minerva back to being mean? Why doesn't she want me to go to cheerleading?

"I thought Bag was helping with cheerleading," Mom says.

"Bag is not helping with cheerleading," Minerva snipes back. "Bag can't help with anything."

I sigh. Looks like things are back to normal. "Fine," I say. "I'll go to your run-through, Mom." There's no way I'm ever going to help Minerva again. If she gets in trouble, it'll be her own fault.

"Are you sure?" Mom asks me.

"Yes," I say.

Then none of us says anything.

Mom's skinny fingers wrap around the steering wheel in a death grip. She's holding so hard that her blue veins and bony knuckles pop out from her skin. Minerva stays quiet. She scoots herself even farther away from me and pushes her body against the door and window.

Seven silent minutes later Mom whips up to the house. She pulls into our driveway and slams on the brakes. The old truck lurches forward and comes to a squeaky stop. Before Mom turns off the engine, Minerva pushes the door open. She's already out of the truck and heading toward the house by the time I scoot away from the dreadful middle seat. I heave myself out of the truck.

With a thud my feet land on rock-solid ground. My toes are cold and stiff, like I'm standing on ice. I look down and realize that ice isn't under my feet. It's dirt, frozen dirt. I see Mom's tire marks etched in the mud from earlier today, her comings and goings, frozen in place. I sigh thinking about how many times Mom must pull in and out of this driveway.

I look away from the frozen mud tracks and breathe in. The freezing air stings my lungs and makes it impossible to take a full breath. Normally I like the cold, but this is too cold. This cold is uncomfortable and extreme, which reminds me of my sister. Everything about her is too much. She's way too cold or way too hot.

Like, inside our house, I'm sure the thermostat is about to be cranked all the way up. It's the first thing Minerva does. She turns that thermostat to eighty. Like the freezing cold, the forced heat is too much. Like my sister, it's all or nothing. We're fighting or we're silent. None of it feels right to me.

I'm about to go inside and make sure Minerva doesn't touch the thermostat, when Mom says, "Give me a hand." I glance into the back of the truck, where four reusable bags are filled to the brim with groceries.

Mom grabs a heavy tote and plops it into my arms.

It's so unfair. Minerva is mean and she doesn't help unload and she never gets in trouble and Mom never asks her to do anything. The front door slams shut as the trace of Minerva's white puffy coat disappears inside. Mom ignores the sound and lifts a heavy grocery tote into her own arms.

"She's getting used to you," Mom says.

"Minerva? She's known me my whole life."

"Getting used to you as a cheerleader."

"I'm not a cheerleader."

"But you are."

Mom grabs the other two tote bags and can barely hold all three in her arms.

"Here." I take one of the totes from her. Now we each hold two.

I follow her inside and feel furious. The cheerleading wasn't my idea. The homework wasn't my idea. Mom's play wasn't my idea. Mom and Minerva do whatever they want and expect me to go along with everything. I drop the grocery bags onto the counter.

"Help me prep tomorrow's meal," Mom says.

She doesn't ask me. She tells me. It's so annoying.

Mom pulls out corn tortillas, avocados, shredded cheese, tomatoes, beans, and chips. The groceries cover every inch of countertop. I wish her theater friends were here to help. But they aren't. It's a ton of food for one person to prepare. Even though I'm mad, I don't want

Mom to make the food alone. Same way I didn't want her to carry the three reusable tote bags alone.

"Enchiladas?" I ask.

"Quesadillas," she says.

Mom spreads the tortillas over the kitchen table, and when the entire table is covered with little yellow circles, she places a handful of cheese on top of each one. I watch her from my spot at the counter. She's still wearing her costume. The wrinkles in her forehead are deep, and she rolls her head in small circles. Her shoulders and neck and back must be hurting again. Every time she rolls her head, she winces. I'm mad, but I also feel sad watching her.

Random Thought 362.2

Feeling mad and sad at the same time is
the worst.

I grab the avocados. "Guacamole?"

"Mash away."

We work side by side. I cut the avocados in half, pop the pits, and scoop the goopy green stuff into a bowl. Mom grabs a bag of chips, and the plastic crinkles in her hands. I hear her opening the bag.

"How did you like cheerleading?" Mom grabs tortilla chips and plops a handful into a Tupperware container.

I shrug.

She scoops up more chips. "Was it fun?"

"The uniform was uncomfortable." I realize I'm still wearing it now, and it feels a tiny bit better. I guess my skin has gotten used to the polyester.

"I think you should go tomorrow. To cheerleading."

I shrug again. There's no way I want to tell her about Minerva. I still don't even know why she got so mad at me.

"Go to cheerleading," Mom says. "My run-through can wait." She keeps scooping up chips. "By the way, how was your drive yesterday? With Dad."

"I don't know."

She scoops more chips from the bag and looks at the containers as she speaks. "Anything can trigger him," she says. "I don't want him to slip."

"Okay," I say.

"Just be aware," she says.

"Okay," I say, even though I'm annoyed. Of course I'm aware. I remember what Minerva told me. That Dad was high. Mom treats me like I don't know anything, but I know a lot.

"You can't be careful enough," she says. "He's very sensitive."

"I get it!" I shout.

Startled by the sound, Mom misses the container and drops the chips. They fall to the floor, and some of the big chips break into tiny chip pieces. She sighs, bends over, and sweeps the pieces back into her hands.

"Sorry," she says to the floor. "I know this is a lot on you. It's a lot on all of us." She tosses the broken chips into the trash.

"Minerva's a lot on me," I whisper.

"She'll come around."

Mom thinks I'm talking about the cheerleading, and right then all I want is to tell her. I want to tell her about the homework and the money and Minerva. I want to tell her I'm worried about Dad.

"Bag," Mom says. "Bag, do you hear me? For the last time, will you turn around and look at me?"

"Huh?" I turn and face her.

"I think you should go to cheerleading. I can come and watch you cheer after my run-through. I'll bring Carl and Cynthia. I'm sure they'll like to watch."

I shrug. "I don't know."

"They'll love it."

There's no way she's going to let me say no.

So I say, "Fine."

Even though what I want to say is, *Minerva was nice for a second but now she's being a jerk and she's in trouble and she's going to make tomorrow awful.*

"Oh goodie!" Mom tells me.

She doesn't understand at all.

I grind my teeth together and turn back to my bowl of avocados. The green mush glistens underneath the bright kitchen light. The color reminds me of the witch's face in *The Wizard of Oz*, and the witch reminds me of Minerva.

Hot air blasts out of the steel radiator next to where I'm standing. I realize Minerva must've cranked the heat. I rush to the thermostat and switch the dial to sixty-five. That'll teach her to mess with the temperature.

Then I head back to the kitchen and grab a fork. I hack into those avocados with arms of steel. I smash and stir and smash and stir, and it feels good to have something to do with my furious hands.

chapter twenty-eight

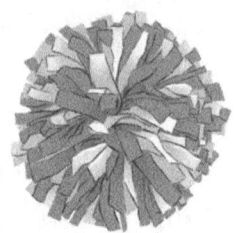

I CAN'T SLEEP. I CAN'T THINK. I CAN'T STAND BEING in my own skin. It's late and I have a bruise on my upper arm where Minerva pinched me and I'm holding it all in and I don't want her secrets anymore. My head rests on my pillow, but it might as well be banging against a brick wall. That's how awful I feel.

I roll over on my bed and look for *The Old Man and the Sea*. The cover peeks out from my backpack and looks even shabbier than before. In addition to the stain from the juice box spill, I notice that the spine is pulling apart at the seams, which makes me feel sick, as if my own spine is pulling apart from my body.

I see another book in my bag. It's the book from Mr. Perkins, *The Wednesday Wars*. The spine is intact, and the hard cover is shiny and new. I grab the book and reread that great first sentence. *Of all the kids in the seventh grade at Camillo Junior High, there was one kid that Mrs. Baker hated with heat whiter than the sun. Me.*

I keep reading, from the beginning, slow and steady. I read and read and read. I read about Holling Hoodhood and Mrs. Baker. I read about Doug Swieteck and Holling's dad. I read about Hoodhood and Associates. I read about Vietnam and Shakespeare and what makes a story a tragedy. When I stop reading, I'm on page seventy-three. It's the most I've ever read in a single sitting. I lean my head back into my pillow.

Seventy-three.

The moment feels enormous, and I don't want to forget it. Even though it's wrong to write in books, and even though it's not even my book to begin with—the book belongs to Mr. Perkins—I take a pencil and lightly circle the number. Then, in tiny lowercase letters, I write "margaret" at the top of the page.

I glance at my clock. 1:42. Holy smokes. 1:42? It's the middle of the night, and I should feel tired, but I don't. I'm the opposite of tired. My eyes are open, my head spins, and my heart pounds inside my chest. I breathe in extra big, but it doesn't help. My heart keeps racing. I'm wired like the inside of a lightbulb about to short-circuit.

I set the book on the table and run my hand across the cover. *The Wednesday Wars.* On the cover I see Holling's red sneakers, a desk, and a shifty rat hiding in the corner. The rat makes me think of Minerva. I look away from the book and stand up. It might be late, 1:43 to be exact, but I don't care. I head straight for her room.

chapter twenty-nine

MY BARE FEET FREEZE IN THE HALLWAY. THE hardwood floor feels cold. I stand motionless in front of her bedroom door. My eyes focus on the floor where a trickle of light spills out from the space between the bottom of the door and the floor.

Why are her lights on? It's almost two in the morning.

Without knocking, I creak the door open.

Minerva sits on top of her perfectly made bed, biting her already-bitten-down nails. She's wearing that beautiful turquoise ring again. It's on her pointer finger. All around her I see money. She's got five-dollar bills and one-dollar bills stacked in neat piles. Her face frowns when I enter. She doesn't look at me. She keeps looking at the money, and her frown turns down further.

"I keep it under my mattress," she says.

"The nine hundred dollars?" I ask.

"The nine hundred and sixty-five dollars, minus the one hundred and ninety-three I gave to Mimi."

"You have to give the money back."

"To Mimi?"

I step inside her bedroom. "To everyone."

Minerva takes the bills and stacks them into one big pile. The pile is perfectly lined up so the presidents face the same way and none of the corners stick out. She keeps stacking bill after bill. "I'm not giving it back."

"If you get caught and you've given it back, you won't get in as much trouble."

"I'm not getting caught."

"Minerva, Mrs. Buttocks knows that someone is doing the homework. She's going to figure out it's you."

"The money's mine," she says. "I earned it."

"What if it becomes mine?" I tilt my head toward her mattress. "I know your hiding spot. What if I take it and give it back for you?"

She narrows her eyes at me. "I dare you."

I hold her gaze.

"What's the money for?" I narrow my eyes at her ring.

"Mom."

"What's it really for?"

She shakes her head.

"I'll stay here all night, Minerva. What's the money for?"

"The questions." She moans. "Can you stop already?"

"Why do you need the money?"

"Mom."

"You keep saying that, but I think you're lying."

"It's for Mom."

"Fine. Then let's go give it to her." I grab a fistful of bills. "Let's go wake her up right now."

"Stop."

"Why?"

"I said STOP!"

Minerva stands up and then she pushes me. She slams her arms into my shoulders, and I stumble back. I almost catch my balance, but then I fall, hard. I let go of the money. My butt slams against the wooden floor, and the money flutters down to meet me. Minerva stares at the mess. The only sound in the room is her heavy breathing.

In, out, in, out.

We wait to hear any indication that we woke Mom up, but the house stays silent and her door stays closed.

"That hurt," I say.

"The money isn't for me," Minerva replies, voice trembling. "It's for Mom . . . and Dad."

"Yeah, right."

Minerva stares at the money on her bed. "The money is for a divorce."

"A divorce?" I shake my head. "Stop lying."

Minerva keeps going. "It's the truth. I'm going to pay for a divorce."

"They don't want a divorce."

"You don't know anything."

"You always say that, and I'm sick of it!" I grab another wad of cash and throw it onto the floor. "I know a lot!"

"Okay, okay." The money spreads around us like snow. She raises her hands as if she's trying to make a truce. "Chill."

Now the room is filled with the sound of my heavy breathing.

In, out, in, out.

I picture the sweater of Dad's that Mom keeps in her closet. She wants him to come back. She doesn't want him to live somewhere else. She's waiting for him to get better.

"They love each other," I say. "They don't want a divorce."

"Honestly, she probably does love him, which is super messed up," Minerva says. "But even if she does, and he loves her, it's not working. She makes him worse. He makes her worse. Look, I heard Mom talking on the phone. It was after Dad moved out, after I saw what I saw. She said she couldn't afford to get a divorce, and that's when I knew I needed to earn money."

"Does she know what you've been doing? With the homework?"

"Of course not."

I picture Mom's writing all over our kitchen walls. *Bag's birthday. Insurance card. Bake sale brownies.* Then I picture Mom's note about Dad. *Call Tom.* What did she want to call him about?

Minerva stares at the money.

I ask, "What did you see?"

"When?"

"Before Dad moved out. You said you saw something."

Minerva begins to gather the money. She doesn't respond to my question. Instead she picks up the bills carefully like she's being graded by how perfect each bill looks.

"They just need a divorce, okay?" she says. "He can't come back."

I don't want to hold this idea in my head, so I bend over and grab a bunch of bills. I grab the money like no one cares how wrinkled it is. Like no matter what it looks like, the bills have the same value. When the bills are cleaned up off the floor, I clutch the money and ask, "Why are you so mad at him?"

Minerva stares at the money, and her eyes look dull, like something just switched off inside. "I'm not mad."

"You seem mad," I say.

The air hangs thick and hot around us. The steel radiator in Minerva's room is inches away from where we're standing. Hot air pours out of it. She must've turned up the temperature again. Minerva. Minerva thinks she knows everything. Minerva thinks she knows what's right. She doesn't. I hate the heat!

Along with the hot air, her words about Dad trickle from my forehead, down my throat, across my heart, and land inside my belly, where they swirl in slow circles and make me feel nauseous. She said he was *high* when he picked me up. Was he high? I thought he was doing the steps. I thought he was talking with his friends. I don't want him to get worse. I don't want them to get a divorce. A divorce means he'll never come back to our house. He won't have his books on the shelves. He won't keep the heat turned down. He won't wear his ironic T-shirts. He won't talk about reading and nature and ice cream and all the things I like.

"You've got to return the money, Minerva."

She looks at me. "Mom and Dad have been in charge, and look where that's gotten them. I'm taking things into my own hands."

I shake my head. "Aren't divorces super expensive?"

"Eddie DiPucchio said a thousand dollars."

"Who?"

"Eddie DiPucchio, attorney-at-law. He said for a thousand dollars he could get anyone divorced. Haven't you seen the signs? They're all over the place. They're on buses and benches. He's wearing a blue suit. He's the real deal. I looked him up on the internet, and it's true. A thousand dollars and he'll get it done." She holds up her cash. "I'm so close. I'll find a way to get the rest."

The bills are wrinkled and crooked and remind me of broken tortilla chips. Even though the money is the same money that was on her bed a moment ago, it now looks completely different.

"Maybe we should talk to Mom," I say.

"Why?"

"I don't know. We can tell her we're worried about Dad."

"No way. Then she's going to want to take care of him, and that will make everything worse. Trust me, Bag. They need a divorce, for both of them. A divorce is the only thing that will make things better."

I sit down on her bed, and a five-dollar bill flutters to the floor. Minerva doesn't pick it up. She sits down next to me, and we stare at the fallen bill like it's a stale tortilla chip neither of us wants to eat. I wonder who gave the bill to her. I wonder where they got it. I wonder if anyone knows that our family is super messed up and that's why Minerva is completing math homework for money. I've got so many questions, and there's no good answer for any of them.

"So, you'll help me?" she says. She motions to the money on her bed.

It's the most money I've ever seen in my whole life. It's probably the most money that's ever been inside this house since we moved in.

"I'm so close to a thousand," she says.

"The money doesn't matter."

"I'm going to get that money."

"And then what? This guy prints out some fancy certificate that says Mom and Dad are divorced? We hang it on the wall, and Mom and Dad live happily ever after, apart? That'll never work. You might be able to earn the money—I'm sure you can—but you can't change them. They are who they are."

"Mr. DiPucchio said so."

"He said what? Did you talk to him?"

"On the phone."

"Minerva. No."

Minerva grabs the five-dollar bill off the floor. "He said he could get the job done. He said don't worry. He said the money would fix everything."

"Money can't fix anything." I shake my head at her. "Minerva, come on. Just look at Mom. She made tons of money when she was on the soap, and they still had the same problems."

"But Mr. DiPucchio said so."

"It sounds like your money is going to fix things for one person. Mr. DiPucchio."

Minerva stares at her hard-earned dollars. She stares at the money as if it was a lost cat she found on the side of the road. She stares at the money as if she doesn't want to see it but can't stop looking.

"He said so," Minerva says. "Mr. DiPucchio said he could help."

"He can't be trusted," I tell her.

"I worked so hard," she whispers. Then Minerva starts to cry. Silent tears roll down her cheeks, one after the other.

"Look." I scoot closer to her and grab her hand.

Her hand feels foreign again, like I'm holding another clump of Silly Putty. It's the second time today that we've held hands. I don't want to let go.

So I keep holding and say, "It's amazing you earned so much, but a divorce isn't going to change them. A divorce is just a piece of paper, and Dad doesn't care about paper and contracts and stuff like that. Dad's just feeling sad. He'll snap out of it."

"I don't think he's snapping out of anything."

"Minerva, what did you see?"

She squeezes my hand tighter. Then she pauses. I wait for her to continue. It feels like she's about to tell me, and I don't want to mess it up. I keep waiting. Finally she says, "I found his stash."

"What?"

"Drugs."

The word hangs above me like a heavy weight pushing me down.

Minerva squeezes my hand again. "Bag, do you know what I'm talking about?"

"Of course," I say. "I know about drugs. I've read *Hey, Kiddo*."

"*Hey, Kiddo?*"

"It's a graphic novel, and the mom character, Leslie, has a serious problem with drugs. I know they can ruin a person's life. But that's not like Dad. I mean, I know he likes to drink beer and maybe, sometimes, he smokes weed. But he's not like *Leslie*."

"It was more than weed."

"Oh."

"His patch is for more than cigarettes."

My heart races. I can feel it pounding in my throat. I want to know, but I don't want to know. I don't want to know what he might be doing.

"Are you okay?" Minerva asks.

We're still holding hands. She gives my hand a little squeeze, and I squeeze back, like we're silently communicating, helping each other with our squeezes. We sit there, and I wonder if she feels sad too. She must feel sad, because she doesn't say anything. She stays quiet. We both stay quiet, still holding hands.

Finally Minerva says, "Mr. DiPucchio guaranteed a divorce."

"You can't guarantee divorces."

"He said I could emancipate or something."

"Minerva, he doesn't care about us. He doesn't care about you."

Her chin quivers. "He's a professional."

"A professional?" I exclaim. "Professionals don't try to scam money from a thirteen-year-old!"

Minerva closes her eyes. Instead of thirteen she looks Mom's age. No. She looks even older. Minerva looks ancient. She looks like the whole world is squishing down her shoulders.

She mutters, "You think I should give back the money?"

"Yes," I tell her. "I think you should give it back."

She presses her lips together like her lawyer friend is not who she thought he was.

Maybe Minerva's not who I thought she was. Maybe she truly loves Dad. Maybe earning the money was her way of loving him, of trying to help him. But no matter how much she earns, it will never be enough. It will never fix him.

My throat burns like lemon juice poured over an open wound. "What if Dad doesn't get better?" I whisper.

Even though I feel terrible for saying that, and for thinking that, it feels true. It feels true to say the most terrible thing to a person who understands.

"I hope he gets better," Minerva says. Then she squeezes my hand one last time before she lets go.

For my whole life I didn't believe we were related. I always thought she was Mom's daughter and I was Dad's daughter and they pretended they'd had us together. But now I know. We're full sisters.

Minerva motions toward the mess of money around us. "Are you one hundred percent sure that if I give the money back, I won't get in trouble?"

"I didn't say you wouldn't get in trouble. I said you wouldn't get in as much trouble."

"I mean, what am I supposed to do? Slip a wad of cash into everyone's locker?"

"Hold on." A plan begins to swirl inside my head. "How does Mimi pass out the homework? Where does she put it?"

"Everyone's lockers," Minerva says. "She said she already put the homework in everyone's lockers during the game."

"Of course." The evidence is still in the lockers. "Get me a pen, paper, and calculator."

"I'm not doing your math homework," she says.

"It's not my homework. I've got an idea."

chapter thirty

THE NEXT MORNING, WE GET TO SCHOOL LATE. Mom forgot her costume after she loaded the lunches, so we had to turn back. Now Mom stops short at the curb, and the lunches in the back of the truck lurch forward.

Minerva glances at me before she opens the door.

I nod.

As promised, I haven't said a word to Mom. As promised, Minerva has the money stashed in the pockets of her puffy white coat.

Minerva hops out of the truck.

Before I'm able to scoot out from the misfortune that is the middle seat, Mom rests her hand on my upper arm. It's the spot where Minerva pinched me yesterday, and it's sore. I flinch away from her.

"Good luck at the game," she says.

With everything going on, with everything that happened last night, I forgot about the game. I forgot about cheerleading.

"I'll come to the game, right after my run-through." Mom looks at me. "I'm proud of you." She looks at Minerva. "I'm proud of both of you."

I slide myself out from the truck. Now I'm standing next to Minerva.

"Girls," Mom says. She keeps the truck running. She waits for us to say something.

She needs to pull away! We need to start our plan! We're already late and the clock is ticking.

"I know this has been a hard year," Mom says, "with me and your dad."

I give a little nod. Mom never talks about anything being hard with them, but things are hard, and I'm glad she says it.

She continues. "I think it's wonderful you've both found cheerleading to sink into. It's important to have things to care about. It's important for all of us. For so many reasons. I meant what I said. I'm very proud. Of both of you."

I don't know what to say.

Right then I want to tell Mom about the money and the homework and the plan to give it back. I don't want to keep secrets from her, but Minerva would be furious at me. So we stand there, me and Minerva, in silence, as Mom glances at the clock on her dashboard. "Dear god," she says. "I'm so late!"

She slides her shifter from park to drive. Minerva slams the passenger door shut.

Minerva and I wave as Mom's truck pulls away from the curb. Mom waves back.

"That was nice," I say. "Saying she's proud of us." My voice catches on the word "proud." I didn't realize how much I liked hearing it.

"It was nice," Minerva says. "But we don't have time to waste."

"Right."

"So, here's your list, and I'm taking this one." She hands me a sheet of paper with six names on it. Her sheet has seven names.

"And the money?" I ask.

Minerva reaches into her puffy coat and pulls out two envelopes. One has my name on it. The other has her name.

"What about Mimi?" I ask.

"I'll talk to Mimi after we finish. First we need to get to every person on our list before school starts."

Minerva holds out her fist. I clench my hand, and my knuckles turn white. Then we pound our fists together.

"See you at lunch," I say. I'm worried about our plan, but I don't want to worry Minerva. So I pretend to be stronger than I feel. "It'll work," I tell her.

Minerva nods and rushes to the front of school while I stay frozen next to the curb and clutch the list of names.

"It has to," I say to the paper.

Then I head for the seventh-grade lockers and prepare to negotiate my first deal. I see Ridgley at his locker. He looks away from me. I want to explain why I was cheering yesterday, that it was my first time, that I was telling him the truth, but I don't have time to talk. I need to get to everyone on the list before school starts! I move past Ridgley.

Random Thought 117
In moments of doubt the only way out
is through.

"Sherman." I stop him before he opens his locker.

Sherman Hughes, the center on the basketball team. His name is the first on my list. Now I know why he wanted to talk to me yesterday. Apparently, he's not a fan of doing math homework. He's paid Minerva more money than anyone else. He looks down at me as if he's standing on a ladder. He's at least a foot taller than me. Possibly two. I grip the sheet in my right hand.

"Yeah?" he finally says. "You want something?"

"Yes, hello, Sherman. I'm here to give you something. Sixty-eight dollars."

"Come on." He shakes his head at me and laughs. "Very funny."

"It's the eighty-five dollars you paid my sister, minus Mimi's cut of seventeen dollars, which brings us to sixty-eight. That's what we can offer."

Sherman doesn't respond.

"You don't need to look surprised." I say. "I know that's why you said hi to me the other day. When you asked if I was working with her."

His eyes turn terrified. "What are you talking about?" The tone of his voice reminds me of a mouse, which is confusing, him being as tall as a giraffe and sounding as small as a mouse. He looks over his shoulder, then looks back at me.

"Not here," he whispers.

"You paid my sister to do your math homework," I say. "Seventeen times."

"No, I didn't."

"Sherman, you did, and I'm not here to get you in trouble. I'm here to cut a deal."

He narrows his eyes. "A deal?"

"You can have the money back," I say.

"For what?"

"I need the math homework that's in your locker."

"That's it?"

"You can't use that homework sheet."

"Did Minerva get busted?"

"Not if you do your own homework and keep quiet."

He nods. I look over my shoulder, reach into my

backpack, take out sixty-eight dollars, and hand it to him. Sherman shoves the money into his pocket.

"Not a word," I say.

"Not a problem," he replies.

Sherman opens his locker. "What the—"

"Where's the homework sheet?" I ask.

Sherman's forehead wrinkles. "It was supposed to be here."

My throat catches.

"What's going on?" he says. "Are you setting me up?"

"Where's the sheet?" Even though he towers above me, my voice stays strong.

"I don't know where the homework sheet is." At the same time, his voice sounds tiny, like he's the one looking up at me. "I swear."

I don't know if I believe him. He's either lying and he's keeping the homework or someone else got to his locker first. Please, please, please let him be lying. *Please, please, please don't let Buttocks have his sheet.*

"Not a word," I say to Sherman.

He nods his head on his stringy neck as a ball of panic knots in the middle of my throat. I swallow and move to the next person on my list.

"Claire," I say. "Claire!"

She's standing at her locker.

I rush over to her.

Claire is a cheerleader. She is very quiet, and she's always stuck at the bottom of the pyramid. She's nice about being on the bottom too. I bet the girls that are bigger than Claire hurt her narrow shoulders when they stand on her. But she never says anything. It must be hard to hold them up and never complain.

"Hi, Bag," Claire says, sounding friendly and shy at the same time.

I cross my fingers for luck. Then I tell her the same thing I told Sherman. She's getting her money back in exchange for: one, the homework sheet, and two, her silence.

"Do we have a deal?" I ask.

"Sure," Claire says. "But Minerva should keep the money."

"What?" I narrow my eyes at her.

"She did the work. It's not fair to take the payment back."

"It's fair," I explain. "As long as you give me the sheet, that's the work Minerva is now paying you for."

I grab cash from my backpack and hold it in front of Claire. She shrugs, takes it. "I guess. But it doesn't seem right."

I watch her move her combination lock to the left, the right, and to the left. The door pops open. Like Sherman's, Claire's locker doesn't have the homework sheet.

My feet feel like blocks of ice stuck to the ground.

"Where's the homework?" she asks.

I zip up my bag, and it feels as though the zipper has caught in my throat and is snagging against my tonsils.

"Are you okay?" Claire asks.

"I'm fine," I mutter. "Please don't say anything, even if Mrs. Buttocks asks you. Please." Then I scoot to find the next person on my list, though I'm certain the homework won't be in their locker either.

chapter thirty-one

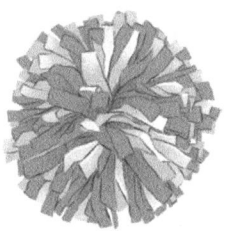

AT LUNCH I FIND MY SEAT AND PLOP DOWN. I arrive before Minerva, and I have no idea how to tell her what happened. How can I say the homework is missing? How can I say I have no idea who has it? I'm too worried to eat, and I leave my guacamole and quesadilla and chips, my Lunch by Lenore, tucked inside the Tupperware.

The clock says 12:05, and Minerva should be here by now. Oh no. What if she got caught? What if she's in the principal's office right now?

Then, finally:

"It's super weird," I hear her say. Minerva plops her Lunch by Lenore onto the table. "I returned the money, but no one had the homework."

"Oh m-my god," I stammer. "I thought you got sent to the principal's office. Wait. Hold on. You know about the missing homework? What happened? Are you sure Mimi put it in the lockers?"

Minerva sits down and opens the lid of her lunch. "Yeah. I'm sure the homework was in there. What happened in math?"

How is she so calm?

"Math was fine," I say in a panicked whisper. "Mrs. Buttocks returned our quizzes, and she said the entire class has a lot of work cut out for them. Then everyone in the class passed in a homework sheet, which they probably did themselves, which was probably all wrong."

Minerva pops a chip into her mouth. "I guess it worked out."

"It didn't work out!" I shove my lunch across the table. "We don't know where the homework is. Thirteen copies, Minerva!" I lean in and lower my voice. "Thirteen copies of your math homework are floating around this school. I don't like it."

I see Mimi's hand before I see her. I see her tiny dark-blue-nail-polished hand on the edge of our cafeteria table.

"Mind if I sit?" she says.

Minerva pops another chip into her mouth. "Yeah, I mind."

"Look." Mimi inches toward Minerva. "I'm sorry for yesterday. I know I was mean. I'm sorry I backed out of our deal."

"I get it." Minerva keeps eating chips like she doesn't have a care in the world. "You got scared. It's cool."

"Mimi," I cut in. "Are you sure you put the homework in the lockers? I couldn't find anyone's sheet."

"I'm sure," she tells me.

"Then why was the homework missing?" I ask.

"Don't know." Mimi unzips her backpack and shoves her small hand inside. She pulls a wad of cash from some secret compartment at the bottom of her bag. Then she holds the money in front of Minerva. I have no idea what is going on.

"Are you serious?" Minerva asks.

"You can have it." Mimi holds the money out to her. "It's the money you paid. One hundred and ninety-three dollars."

"I don't want it," Minerva says.

"Me neither." Mimi's hand trembles as she holds the wad of cash.

"Would you put that away?" I point to her backpack. "What are you trying to do, Mimi? Get us completely busted? Where is the homework?"

Mimi reaches way down into the depths of her backpack and hides the money. "Sorry," she says to Minerva.

"You're the one who quit," Minerva says. "Why are you acting like I fired you?"

Mimi pulls her hand out from her backpack, and her

miniature shoulders cave in toward one another. "I guess I felt like I got replaced."

"By who?"

"Her." Mimi points to me.

Minerva tilts her head. "Are you serious?"

Mimi continues, "I thought we were friends, and then Bag comes along and totally takes my place. She took my place in cheerleading. She took my place with the homework. She took my place with you."

Minerva stops eating her chips. "No, she didn't. It's just that . . . she's my sister."

"Yeah, well, I don't have one of those, either."

Mimi thinks I'm taking Minerva away from her? Little does Mimi know, we might be sisters, but Minerva doesn't like me. She still makes fun of me constantly.

The table is silent, and I wonder if Minerva is going to say that having a sister stinks. Instead Minerva gives Mimi a small smile. "I guess I'm pretty lucky."

I don't believe it. I stay frozen with my mouth open so big that I feel like the whole Tupperware container could fit inside.

"I still want to be friends," Minerva says to Mimi.

"Me too," Mimi replies.

Minerva passes over her quesadilla as Mimi's dark blue nails reach for the cheesy triangle. The food exchanges from Minerva's hand to Mimi's, and I notice something. Minerva is wearing that ring again. The ring is turquoise and gold and beautiful. The ring is on her pointer finger.

"Yum!" Mimi exclaims. She now holds Minerva's quesadilla in her right hand. "Grilled cheese is my favorite."

Minerva doesn't correct her, which is how I know that Minerva's not mad at her. There's no way Minerva would let a mistake like that slide if she was. She'd say "quesadilla" super slow.

"Yum is right," Minerva tells her, and pops another chip into her mouth.

My eyes return to that ring. The gold edges sparkle, and the turquoise middle is smooth and round. I narrow my eyes.

"Where did you get that?" I point to her finger.

Minerva stares at me, then quickly glances down at the table.

"Where did you get the ring?" I ask.

"I don't know," Minerva mumbles. Then she shoves some chips into her mouth, so she doesn't have to answer.

The smell of cod wafts into my nose. Something's fishy, and not just the hot lunch. I look at Minerva. I look at Mimi.

"Are you guys not telling me the whole truth here? Did you buy that ring?" I ask Minerva.

"No," she says.

"Where is the homework, Mimi?"

"Don't know," she says. "I promise."

I stare at the ring and worry that Minerva bought the ring using her homework money. I worry she's been lying to me. What if she didn't return the money? What if she's saving it to buy stuff? What if she and Mimi are working together behind my back?

Minerva and Mimi continue to eat their quesadilla and chips. They talk about cheerleading practice. They talk about getting new uniforms with pockets. They talk about gum.

"Are you sure the homework was inside the lockers?" I ask Mimi again.

"I'm sure." She dunks her quesadilla into the guacamole.

chapter thirty-two

SURPRISINGLY, THE REST OF THE SCHOOL DAY GOES by without a problem.

Like I told Minerva at lunch, Mrs. Buttocks didn't mention anything in math. Mrs. Buttocks asked everyone to pass in their homework. Everyone passed in their own sheet. The missing sheets haven't turned up. But the day is not over. I have no idea where Minerva got that ring, I don't know where the homework is, and I still have one more class, advanced English with Mr. Perkins.

"Dude." In the hallway someone pulls on my backpack, and I turn around. Sherman Hughes shakes his head. "Come on, Bag, move. You're in the way."

I look over my shoulder, look back at Sherman. "Did you find the homework sheet?" I whisper.

"No."

"It never turned up?"

"No."

"Have you seen my sister today?"

"No."

"Do you think Mrs. Buttocks knows about the homework?"

He shrugs. "Don't think so."

He heads down the hall with his shoulders slumped forward. It makes no sense why nobody seems to be worried about this. Counterfeit homework is a really big deal! My eyes move away from Sherman and focus on Mr. Perkins's room.

I'm standing in the hallway. I glance inside. Mr. Perkins sits at his wooden desk covered with a mess of papers and coffee cups and gum wrappers. He isn't wearing his tweed blazer. Instead the blazer hangs behind him.

I step into his room. Mr. Perkins stays at his desk.

To get to my seat, I pass Ridgley and search his eyes for a friendly glance, but he ignores me. It's so frustrating! We went from friends to not friends overnight.

"Ridgley." I pause at my desk. "We can't even say hi anymore?"

"Hi," he says.

"Are we seriously fighting because I was wearing a cheerleading uniform? Why are you so mad about me cheerleading?"

"It's not about cheerleading." He pulls the collar of his T-shirt away from his neck. "I mean, we're not fighting."

"Then why are you acting weird?"

"I'm not acting weird."

"Things seem weird."

"It's just that . . ."

"It's just what?"

"Nothing. I mean, not here."

BLAHHH! The late bell sounds above me like a fire alarm.

"Come on, Bag." Mr. Perkins stands up from his desk. "Take a seat," he says to me.

Then he begins his lesson.

Not surprisingly, I'm not able to pay attention. Why won't Ridgley look at me? What does he mean, "not here"? Why is nothing in my life making sense right now? Why? Why? Why?

Mr. Perkins is talking about poetry again. He says a few words, pauses, says a few more words. Pauses. The way he speaks sounds like music. Even though I'm barely listening, and I have no idea what the poem is about, I like the pauses. I like the rhythm. I like the space between the words.

Random Thought 811

I wish stories had as much white space
as poems. It would make reading so
much easier.

I stare at the sheet in front of me. Mr. Perkins must have passed the sheets out at the beginning of class. I don't remember getting one, but here it is. It's a sheet that's titled SUMMER with a list of words on it.

>Honey
>Pebble
>Toast
>Tadpole
>Bubble gum
>Banana
>Bowling ball
>Shoelace
>Anthill
>Swing
>Peanut butter
>Bare feet
>Berries

"Bag."

Huh? I realize that someone is saying my name.

"Bag." Mr. Perkins looks at me from his desk. "Do you have a word to add?"

"Add to what?"

Mr. Perkins sighs. He picks up a copy of the sheet from his desk. "Do you have any words to add?"

"About summer?"

He nods.

I panic because his nod isn't friendly. His nod is annoyed that I haven't been paying attention, and now I can't think of a word.

"Uh," I stumble. "Deodorant?"

The class bursts into laughter.

Mr. Perkins's face is blank.

"I wasn't trying to be funny," I explain.

The class keeps laughing.

Mr. Perkins looks away from me and calls on someone else for a summer word. I'm upset, and I don't look at the person he calls on. I still don't look as someone in the room says "ocean." Instead I close my eyes and wait for class to end.

Deodorant. How could I?

> **Random Thought 612.9**
> The expression "put your foot in your mouth" isn't enough. It should be worse. Like "put your thumb in your mouth" or "put your butt in your mouth." Yeah. That's exactly what I just did. I put my butt in my mouth.

At the end of class Mr. Perkins calls me over.

"Can we talk?" he says.

I don't respond, because I don't want to talk. But it's not like I have a choice after having put my butt in my mouth. My feet drag in slow motion as I inch toward his desk. The rest of the class has already left the room.

"Sorry," I say to the floor, and my voice totally catches.

"Sorry for what?" he asks.

"Sorry for saying 'deodorant.'"

I look up. The ceiling is made of Styrofoam panels, and there's a spitball stuck to the square Styrofoam panel above where I stand.

"I didn't call you over because you're in trouble," he says.

I keep staring at the ceiling. "I wasn't trying to be funny," I mumble. "It was the first word I thought of."

"Now, now," he replies. "It's a fair word for summer. I just didn't want to make a big deal about it and get the class even more riled up."

Oh no. If I'm not in trouble for saying "deodorant," am I in trouble for the counterfeit homework? Does he know? How could he know? Oh no, oh no. Does he think it was me?

My eyes look away from the ceiling and find Mr. Perkins. Which makes me feel embarrassed, so I look at the floor.

"I just want to know if everything is okay." He speaks in a soft voice. "You seem distracted," he adds.

I don't know what to say to him. I keep looking at the

floor, and words tumble out of my mouth, unplanned.

"My sister is saving money for a lawyer for a divorce," I hear myself telling him. "For our parents. Either that or she's a total liar."

He nods, and his nod isn't like the annoyed nod he gave me after he caught me spacing out. The nod is slow and gentle. It's the kind of nod a person gives when they understand.

"Do you want to talk about it?" he asks.

I don't know how to talk about it because I don't know what's true and what's not true. So I say the most honest thing I can think of.

"I don't know."

"Fair enough." Mr. Perkins keeps nodding. Then he asks, "How's *The Wednesday Wars* coming?"

"Oh." I focus my eyes on his freshly shaved face. So I guess he doesn't know about the homework. "Good," I say. "Really good. I'm on page seventy-three."

I pause on the number and let myself feel important. Seventy-three.

"That's great," he says. "What do you like most about the story so far?"

"I like Holling and I want him to stand up to his family, and I think his friend Doug is a good guy, and yeah. It's a good book."

"Glad to hear it," Mr. Perkins says.

I realize the game is about to start. Minerva will be

there with the cheerleaders. I need to find out about that ring. I need to know if everything she told me was untrue.

"Gotta go," I say quickly.

"See you, Bag." Mr. Perkins smiles, and his cheeks move up near his eyes, and for a tiny moment it seems as though everything might work out, until I remember, nothing is working out.

chapter thirty-three

I STUMBLE OUT OF HIS CLASSROOM. THE HALLWAY is loud and crowded and filled with people and their backpacks and their cell phones and their skateboards and their fist bumps. I step back, but someone pushes me forward. It feels like I'm stuck inside an overstuffed piñata. I've got to get to the storage closet.

"The game starts in twenty minutes!" someone says.

"It's the finals!" another person says.

Every person in school zips through the hallway like we're tiny bits of candy flying from ripped papier-mâché. I maneuver past the excitement and head straight for the storage closet, straight for the cheerleaders, straight for my sister.

Oddly enough, when I get to the storage closet, Minerva isn't here. Neither is Mimi. I see Emily C.,

Emily S., Claire.... The cheerleaders slide on uniforms, apply makeup, and tie their hair into ponytails.

"Twenty minutes until game time!" someone says.

Someone else says, "Hurry up, Bag! Get on your uniform!"

I do not put on my uniform. I leave it in my backpack. Then I tap Emily S. on the shoulder. "Have you seen my sister?"

She shrugs.

I ask Emily C., who is standing next to her, "Have you?"

She shrugs.

I ask Claire, "Do you know where Minerva is?"

"I don't," she says.

"Was she here earlier?"

"She wasn't."

"Do you know where she is?"

"Sorry, Bag. I don't."

I wish Claire had answers for me, but I do appreciate that she uses her words instead of shrugging. "Thanks," I say.

Then I leave the storage closet and go to the one place where I think Minerva might be. I fly down the hall, through the cafeteria, and out the side door. I stand in front of the dumpsters. The area is empty and smells like trash. My sister isn't here.

I feel so discouraged. If she isn't at cheerleading, and

she isn't at the dumpsters, where is she? I have a terrible feeling creep from my stomach, up my chest, and land in my throat. I'm worried something very bad has happened to my sister.

What if she didn't buy that ring? What if she stole it? What if she was telling the truth about the divorce? What if she contacted that lawyer guy? What if she gave him some of the money? What if it wasn't enough? What if he wanted more?

The what-ifs fill my brain like a balloon. My brain is so full, it feels close to popping. I stumble away from the dumpsters and head to the front of school, to the sidewalk, to the place where Mom usually drops us off. I know Mom's not going to be here, but it's where my day started with Minerva. Maybe Minerva will be at our drop-off place too? I race to the curb.

Not surprisingly, when I get to the curb, Mom's truck isn't here. Unfortunately, neither is Minerva. I see other families, other cars, other parents picking kids up from school. Minerva is nowhere in sight.

I slump down and sit on the curb because I don't know what else to do with myself. I don't want to cheer. I don't want to watch the game. I don't want to do anything other than find my sister and figure out what's going on.

I stay sitting on the cold curb, waiting. My backpack stays on my back, holding my books and my cheerleading uniform. The slow roll of tires surrounds me. Doors open and close, engines remain running, the smell of car exhaust fills my nose. Adult voices say, "Hey, buddy! How was your day?

"I'm so happy to see you!"

"How was the spelling test?"

"Did you eat your lunch?"

Mostly it's the parents who speak, and every so often a kid says:

"Okay."

"I guess."

"Yeah."

"Maybe."

Then the voices stop. The roll of car tires grows faint. The opening and closing of doors goes away. I stay on the curb and drop my head onto the arms of my jacket. I keep my face hidden in the fabric. My fake glasses press into the bridge of my nose. I smell lavender and bubble gum and the hint of a dusty attic. Then I hear the sound of an engine. Wheels roll on the pavement.

I look up and see a minivan. The minivan is brand-new and white with ski racks on top. The minivan has a dad behind the wheel, a mom in the passenger seat, and three kids in the back.

The minivan drives past me, and I stare at the back of the car. The license plate is from Rhode Island, Mom's favorite, a light blue wave. The minivan continues down the road. Now I'm completely alone.

I can't stop thinking about Minerva. I feel totally helpless. No one even knows I'm sitting on this curb by myself. I don't think I've ever felt so alone. I wonder if this is how my dad feels in his new place. I cover my face with my arms and let myself cry big, fat tears into my fake glasses.

After a few deep breaths I stop crying. I take off my glasses. They're foggy and wet. So I wipe them with the bottom of my jacket. Then I put my glasses back on and notice, on the ground, near the curb, a wrinkled five-dollar bill. I wonder if it belongs to Minerva. I wonder if she dropped it this morning.

Even though the glasses have never helped my vision, even though the glasses aren't helping me see the money, it's like I can see something I couldn't see before.

No matter what she did, even if she lied to me, Minerva needs help. I'm not giving up on my sister.

chapter thirty-four

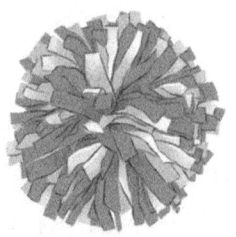

I STAND UP, AND MY LEGS ARE SHAKY AS I WALK to the entrance of the gym. I can't stop shivering. I move toward the gym because I need to find Minerva.

As I get closer to the entrance, a pounding sound explodes from the inside. I love the way it sounds. I move closer and realize it's the sound of the basketballs smacking on the floor, feet stomping against the bleachers, and hands clapping together, excited for the final basketball game to begin.

The pounding continues, and I get the most amazing idea. I remember the cheerleaders with their makeup and their uniforms and their big, thick hairbrushes pulling their hair into ponytails.

"Hairbrushes," I say to no one, because I'm standing outside the gym, alone.

Then I scoot inside and head straight for the storage closet, hoping Minerva is there. My eyes scan the closet, looking for my sister. The room is filled with cheerleaders and chatter. My sister isn't here.

Where is Minerva? My chest hurts, like my heart wants to push up out of my throat. The cheerleaders are fighting about what cheer to start with. Everyone wants something new, but no one has any ideas.

I ask, "Does anyone know where Minerva is?"

My eyes scan the room. I realize that in addition to Minerva, Mrs. Yoh is also missing.

"We need a new cheer," someone says.

"Totally," someone else says.

"Minerva should be here any minute," another voice says.

I decide to wait. It would be foolish to look for her somewhere else if she's on her way here.

"Ugh!" another voice says. "We need a new cheer!"

So in a small voice I say, "I have an idea."

The cheerleaders all move toward me.

I say, "Pick up a hairbrush. Everyone." I slam my hand against the floor as if I was holding a brush myself. "It's a one-two-three count," I say. I slam my hand into the floor again, and the cheerleaders copy me, with their brushes.

A beat keeps forming in my head. It thumps and pauses like a poem, like a song, like a cheer that will get everyone on their feet.

"Claire, you tap, tap, tap like this. Slow and steady."

"Emily S., you can keep going with the hairbrush like this." I tap faster.

"And everyone else . . ." I whack my hand against the floor. "Tappity, tappity, tappity, tappity. . . ."

The cheerleaders fall into rhythm. The beats work together and make an incredible chanting sound.

Claire says, "This should be our first cheer!"

Someone else says, "Two minutes until game time!"

"WOO-HOO!" The cheerleaders line up with their hairbrushes and race out of the room.

I may not know much, like where my sister is and why she keeps disappearing, but I do know I made up a cheer, and the cheerleaders want to do it. So I take my uniform out of my backpack, undress, drop my backpack and clothes in a messy pile in the storage closet. Then I pull my uniform over my head and . . .

The tight collar knocks off my glasses. Ugh!

I bend over to pick up my glasses. One of the lenses is cracked. I put the glasses on, and the cracked part makes my vision all wobbly. So I take the glasses off, toss them toward my backpack, turn to leave the storage closet, and smack right into her. Our eyes meet. It's Minerva.

"I'm in so much trouble," she says.

She's wearing a uniform, but she looks disheveled. Her top is backward, and her normally sleek hair isn't pulled into a ponytail. It's long and wild.

"Where have you been?" I ask. "Are you okay? I went to the dumpsters, the curb . . ."

"Mrs. Yoh wants to talk to me! After the game!"

"About what? Are you sure you're in trouble?"

Minerva grabs my hand and pulls me out of the storage closet. "Quick! We can't be late for cheering." Then she begins sprinting toward the gym, pulling me right along with her.

chapter thirty-five

SECONDS LATER I'M SITTING WITH THE CHEERLEADERS on the floor beside the basketball court. The bleachers are behind us. Mrs. Yoh is nowhere in sight. In addition to Mrs. Yoh, Mimi also appears to be missing. The cheerleaders are fighting.

"Not that one."

"I like the cheer called 'Crush.'"

"I like 'Booty, Booty, Booty.'"

"I think we should do Bag's hairbrush cheer."

"No way! We should start with 'Game Time.'"

Without Mrs. Yoh, there is no order. Every cheerleader wants to do something different. No one is agreeing.

A buzzer sounds, and the basketball players huddle together.

"We've got to do something!" Claire says.

Minerva leans in. Her hair is pulled back into a ponytail, but her top is still backward. "Listen up!" she shouts. The girls quiet down and look at her. "We'll do the pyramid first. Everyone, get to your places. Now!"

The cheerleaders hop up.

Minerva puts her hand on my shoulder. "You're the top."

"But . . ."

"We need you," she replies. "Mimi is usually the top. I don't know where she is."

Minerva drags me to the middle of the court. I feel silly wearing the uniform. I feel nervous about the pyramid. I've never been in a pyramid, let alone on the top! I have no idea what I'm doing.

I move my hand to push my glasses up the bridge of my nose and remember that I broke my glasses. I'm not wearing them. Which makes me feel even worse, wearing this uniform, standing in front of a crowd, without my glasses.

The crowd stares at me. There are over a hundred people in the gym. I see familiar faces and unfamiliar faces. Students and teachers and parents from our school and the school our team is playing against. Mrs. Yoh has returned. She's standing in front of the bleachers, cheering us on, a few feet away from the court.

Then my eyes stop at the bottom bleacher near the door.

It's my mom.

Mom looks like her old self, her New York self, her soap-star self. She wears makeup and her hair is fluffy. She's got her shirt tucked into a pair of high-waist pants. She looks great. Carl and Cynthia sit next to her. The three of them are smiling. Carl wears a suit. Cynthia wears a red dress. The three of them look like movie stars.

A line from Mom's play pops into my mind. It's the one she's been saying over and over. *Everyone has something good about them.*

Maybe Mom was practicing the line so much because she wanted me to hear it. Maybe she kept saying the line over and over because she wants me to know there's something good about me too. I get a warm feeling right in the middle of my chest.

Mom turns to her left, and I notice, on the other side of her, it's Ridgley.

"Ridgley!" I get the urge to wave at him, but then I feel silly. Things are still weird between us. So I look away from Ridgley, and then, several rows behind my mom, I see him.

Dad.

Why is he here? Did Mom tell him to come? Why aren't they sitting together?

He's wearing a bright blue hoodie that's unzipped. His face is handsome, covered in brown stubble, with his wide mouth and easy grin, but his eyes. His eyes aren't here. His brown eyes are looking at me, but it's like he's not really looking at me. He reminds me of a ghost, like there's nothing underneath the sheet that covers him.

I notice he's wearing a T-shirt under the hoodie. The T-shirt says GARLIC BREAD, and there's a big picture of garlic bread covered with butter and garlic and parsley and parmesan cheese. The garlic bread looks delicious. I love the T-shirt.

Dad keeps his eyes on me. I realize he came to the gym to watch me. I bet Mom told him about the game, about me being a cheerleader. He gives me a little nod, as if he's telling me I can do it. Maybe Dad doesn't always take care of himself, but I know, in this small moment, he's trying to take care of me.

I stay looking at my dad. Even if he isn't sitting with my mom, even if his eyes look a little lost, he's still my dad. I nod back.

Then I feel a hand on my shoulder. It's Minerva.

"Bag," she says.

I look beyond her. We're standing in the middle of the court, in the middle of the cheerleaders, in the middle of everything. The gym falls silent.

Everyone stares at us.

Then Minerva lifts me off the floor. She helps me climb to the top. Her hands stay on me with every step I take. I step on Claire's back as Minerva lifts me higher.

Finally I'm kneeling on Emily S. and Emily C. I'm the top of the pyramid.

Not a moment later Minerva claps her hands. Then she lands in a full split in front of our pyramid. Her hands are lifted in the air.

"Ta-da!" she yells.

The crowd goes wild. I feel like I've climbed a whole mountain. I feel so good, I don't want to think about all the bad stuff that's happened today. I start shouting words I wish we were cheering.

"Give it your best! Go, team! Everyone is in it together!"

The crowd bursts into more applause.

Someone shouts, "Go, Bag!"

The buzzer sounds.

Minerva stands from her split and helps me climb down from the pyramid. The basketball players run onto the court. The basketball game begins. I rush to the side, and for the first time ever, I feel like a cheerleader.

Random Thought 791.6
It's not so bad, being at the top of a
pyramid, saying all those helpful words.

chapter thirty-six

THE GAME FLIES BY. WE DO THE "BOOTY, BOOTY, Booty" cheer. I don't know the words, so I just clap along. We do the cheer where I'm having a fight with Minerva. Everyone laughs. We do the hairbrush cheer. Everyone loves it.

The buzzer rings. The game ends.

Our team wins!

The cheerleaders burst into applause.

The crowd bursts into applause.

We hug each other, me and Minerva, Emily S., Emily C., Claire. We all hug each other, rush off the court, and head to the storage closet.

"We won!" Claire exclaims.

It feels great, like I'm part of something wonderful. My heart feels light and fluttery, and my cheerleading uniform doesn't itch at all.

But then we get to the storage closet.

Minerva's face is pale. She stands near the door. She looks at the floor. Mrs. Yoh is right by her side, frowning and holding a clipboard. I remember Minerva saying that Mrs. Yoh wanted to speak with her at the end of the game. Mimi is also in the storage closet.

Oh no, oh no, this can't be good.

"We need to talk, Minerva," Mrs. Yoh says in a serious voice. "Right now."

What does she want to talk about?

"Bag, Mimi, you too," she adds.

Oh no, oh no, oh no. I turn to Minerva. Her face is stone cold, like she's more of a statue than a person. She doesn't say a word. Mrs. Yoh steers me, Minerva, and Mimi toward the hallway.

Then she pops her head back into the storage closet and announces to the cheerleaders, "Girls, you did a marvelous job! Great work!"

She clutches her clipboard and rushes out of the storage closet. She clomps toward us at the end of the hall, unclips a stack of paper from her clipboard, and snaps the clip back into place, as if she's performing a rhythm of her own. The papers crinkle in her grip.

Before she says a word, I know we're toast. We're done. The worst thing is about to happen. I know because the papers Mrs. Yoh holds in her hand are Minerva's counterfeit homework.

chapter thirty-seven

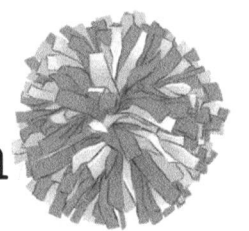

MRS. YOH LOOKS AT ME, AND IT'S LIKE SHE knows all the stuff. Not just the homework stuff, all the stuff. She knows I'm dyslexic. She knows my dad moved out. She knows my family is completely messed up.

She keeps looking at me, and I want to hide under an enormous pile of pom-poms and twist the plastic strings around my wrists and ankles and shove the handle into my mouth, so I never have to speak or move again.

Mrs. Yoh turns the papers around, so they face Minerva. At the sight of the homework, Minerva's face goes as white as the sheets of paper.

Mrs. Yoh holds the homework in front of us like a lawyer in a courtroom. "Who would like to begin?"

Minerva shifts in her sneakers.

I stay as stiff as a statue.

Mimi picks at her tiny blue nails.

"I can't believe you did it," Minerva says to Mimi.

"I didn't do anything. You're the one who was doing something bad."

"You helped me!"

"You made me!"

"We were friends!"

"Now, now, girls," Mrs. Yoh cuts in. "I've got to tell you, when Mimi first brought me these papers—"

"Unbelievable," I say. "Mimi, you lied! You said you put them into the lockers!"

I'm not sure why I say it. Maybe it's because I've known all along that Mimi would turn us in. Maybe I was just waiting for a moment to say it out loud. Maybe it's because I don't want to pretend anymore.

Random Thought 302.2
Sometimes there's nothing left but the
truth.

"So, the thing is," I say to Mrs. Yoh, "Minerva did the homework, but no one turned in that homework. Everyone turned in their own math homework today. I know that for a fact. So really, when you think about it, nothing bad happened."

"That's right, Mrs. Yoh," Minerva says. "No one used that homework today."

"Girls, girls." Mrs. Yoh holds the sheets in the air. "Mimi told me everything."

Minerva glares at Mimi. "Traitor."

Mimi can't look at Minerva. She keeps picking at her tiny blue nails.

"Are we in trouble?" I ask.

"Now, now." Mrs. Yoh fans her face with the homework. "I've been thinking about this quite a lot. My first reaction was to go straight to Principal Doonesbury, and I've got to tell you, part of me still wants to do that because I believe in fairness and I believe actions have consequences. But on the other hand, I do realize there are two sides to every story. You must've had a very good reason to help kids with their homework, and I'm thrilled that Mimi came to me for help. So really, what this incident boils down to is teamwork."

"Teamwork?" Minerva and I say together.

"Yes, forging homework was a very bad idea. And yes, if you hadn't tried to right your wrongs by stopping the cheating and returning the money, you'd be having this conversation with Principal Doonesbury. But the truth is, you helped each other work through this on your own. You had a change of heart and, without external pressure, decided to do the right thing. As they say, character is doing the right thing when nobody is looking."

"Hold on," I say. "Minerva and I worked together,

but Mimi didn't." I picture the cafeteria, Mimi's blue nails, the wad of cash she slipped back into her backpack. "Not all of the money was returned."

"That's right!" Minerva says. "Bag is telling the truth!"

It feels good, Minerva standing up for me.

"Mimi still has one hundred and ninety-three dollars," Minerva adds.

"Indeed," Mrs. Yoh says. "Mimi told me about that, too."

"She did?" Minerva and I say at the same time.

Mrs. Yoh nods. "Mimi didn't know what to do about the money. She wanted to give it back to you. So instead we thought we might donate it to a good cause."

Mimi nods.

Mrs. Yoh continues, "But we haven't had time to come up with anything. Any ideas?"

Minerva, Mimi, and I all get quiet. I think about waiting in Mrs. Yoh's car. I think about how kind she is, how enthusiastic she is, how she's always nice even when things aren't ideal. I realize how much I like Mrs. Yoh.

"Maybe we could start a cheerleading fund," I say.

"That's a great idea," Mrs. Yoh says in her typical cheerful voice. "But we've got a sizeable fund already from the PTO. I was thinking more along the lines of people who need the money. Perhaps the Salvation Army?"

I love the Salvation Army. It's where all my favorite T-shirts come from. It's where my mom shops. It's probably where my dad shops too.

"Yes," Minerva says. "I think we should do that."

"Me too," I say. "We also need to get the other money back. The money I gave to Sherman and Claire and the others. We can give that to the Salvation Army too."

"Good thinking," Minerva says.

"Mimi?" Mrs. Yoh says. "Sound good to you?"

"Yes, sounds good." Her voice is small and timid. "But . . ." Mimi's voice sounds so tiny, like she's barely able to get the words out. "You said I could be head cheerleader, Mrs. Yoh."

"Good heavens, did I?" Mrs. Yoh waves her clipboard in front of her face.

Minerva frowns. "What?"

Mimi looks down at the floor. She can't look at Minerva.

Minerva turns to Mrs. Yoh. She's still frowning, but she says, "Mimi deserves it. She's the one who's been writing the cheers."

Mrs. Yoh looks right at Minerva. "I appreciate you telling me that, Minerva, and yes, in that case, I agree. I think Mimi should be captain."

Mimi smiles.

"And, Bag," Mrs. Yoh continues. "I'd like you to be part of the squad too. Permanently."

I nod, slowly at first, then more firmly. I look at Minerva. I don't mind the idea of being a part of something—with my sister.

"Yay!" Cheering erupts from the storage closet.

Mrs. Yoh faces the closet. "Oh my, why aren't they packing up already?" She leaves us and rushes toward the storage closet.

We turn to follow, and Minerva grabs Mimi's wrist, Minerva's ring flashing.

"Not so fast," Minerva says.

Mimi looks at her.

Minerva leans in closer. "Why did you lie to me about the homework? Why did you turn me in to Mrs. Yoh? That wasn't cool. Was it just to be head cheerleader? You should've just said that."

"I mean, I do want to be head cheerleader, but . . ." Mimi looks at me and then back at Minerva. "But it's more than that."

"More than what?"

"I don't know. You hurt my feelings. Like I said before, you were spending so much time with Bag. It felt like you didn't want to be my friend anymore."

"Of course I want to be your friend. I mean, I want to be your friend if you promise not to rat me out. Ever again."

"I won't, Minerva. I promise." Mimi looks at me,

then Minerva. "It was cool how you gave everyone back the money. And it was cool you helped too, Bag. And I like the Salvation Army idea."

"It feels like the right thing to do," Minerva says.

"I agree," I say.

Then Minerva and Mimi stare at the floor. In the silence the air around us warms, like a soup simmering on gentle heat.

"Friends?" Mimi asks.

"Friends," Minerva replies.

They both look at me. I thought they were only asking each other.

"Friends," I say.

Before Mimi turns to go, she catches herself. "Oh hey. I never figured it out. What was all that money for?" Mimi asks Minerva. "Why did you need so much?"

Minerva doesn't respond.

I motion to her hand. "You didn't return all the money, did you? You used some of the money to buy that ring. It's okay if you did. We'd understand."

"I returned all the money," she says.

"Where did you get the ring, Minerva?"

Minerva presses her lips together, then says, "It's from Mom, okay? Don't you remember? When she took me to Ryan's Arcade for my birthday. Well, we passed this jewelry shop in the mall, and I saw the ring and it was so beautiful, and even though Mom couldn't afford it, she bought it for me. For my birthday."

"Oh." I look back at the ring.

"I didn't tell you because I didn't want to rub it in. I know going to Ryan's was my present, and I thought it would hurt your feelings."

"Wow," I say. "Thanks."

"That's why I wore it when I was alone, because I didn't want you to see it. But then, after you did see, I started to wear it because I think it's really pretty."

"It is," I say. "Super pretty." But what I'm really saying is more than that. What I'm really saying is, I understand. Minerva returned the money. She did a very good thing. In more than one way.

Mimi links arms with Minerva. "Your nails are cute," Minerva says.

The three of us head toward the storage closet.

"It's Midnight Sky," Mimi says.

"I love the color," Minerva says.

"Blue is my favorite color," I add.

"Okay, girls!" Mrs. Yoh claps her hands inside the storage closet. "Let me introduce you to our new head cheerleader!"

Mimi does a little jump. Then she joins Mrs. Yoh and the rest of the team in the storage closet.

Minerva and I hang back.

"Let's find Mom," I say.

Before Minerva responds, a motorcycle boot squeaks against the linoleum floor at the end of the hallway. It's Ridgley.

chapter thirty-eight

RIDGLEY STANDS IN THE HALLWAY. HE BEGINS to walk toward me. He's wearing a white T-shirt, and he's holding an empty coat hanger. When he gets close to where I'm standing, he stops.

"Um," he says, "hi."

"Hi," I say.

Minerva clutches her hands to her chest. "Aw. So cute."

I motion to the hanger in Ridgley's hand. "What's going on?"

He shrugs. "It's from Mr. Perkins's room. I'm going to return it."

"Why do you have it?"

He shoves one of his hands into his pocket, the hand not holding the hanger. "I know I messed up. I should've been honest with you from the beginning, and I wanted to make it up to you. So this morning I went to school early, to get the homework out from the lockers."

He holds up the hanger.

"Hold on, what?"

He keeps going. "I got to school early. I was trying to fish the homework out of the lockers, but then Mimi came up to me and told me there was nothing to worry about."

"How did you know about the homework?"

"I've been paying attention, Margaret. I pay attention to what you do. I wanted to help you, even if you couldn't ask for it yourself."

"But why?" I say. "Why would you put yourself in the middle of all this trouble?"

Ridgley moves toward me until he's standing a foot away. Still he won't look at me. "Because . . ." Ridgley keeps looking at the floor.

"I think I know," Minerva says.

Finally, Ridgley looks at me. It's like Minerva didn't say anything. He keeps his eyes right on mine. "Because . . . I like you. I mean, I like you as a friend. But I like you as more than a friend, too."

He looks back at the floor. "I was trying to tell you that the other day. That's why I got upset about Sherman. Because I wanted you to like me. I thought . . . I thought maybe now that you were getting into cheerleading, things would change between us."

"Oh." Now my face feels flushed, and my heart beats a trillion miles a minute. "I like you. I mean, I like you as a friend, and . . ." I take a big breath. "More than a friend."

He takes a step closer to me. He speaks so softly, I can barely hear him. "You're not wearing your glasses."

I forgot I wasn't wearing them.

"My glasses cracked," I say.

The moment I say it, I realize that Ridgley doesn't know. He knows they're not real. But Ridgley doesn't know why I wanted to wear glasses in the first place.

"You look pretty," he says. "I mean, you look pretty with your glasses, too." His face flushes. He stops talking.

I take a huge breath because I want to tell him the truth even though it's uncomfortable. I want Minerva to know too. I don't want to hide who I am. "You know the other day, how I said I didn't need glasses? Well, I don't need them. I was wearing them because they made me feel smart, because most of the time I don't feel that way."

"I think you're very smart," Ridgley says.

"I'm dyslexic," I say.

The word lands softly around us.

Ridgley nods, like he doesn't mind at all. Minerva gives me a little smile, like it doesn't bother her, either.

Ridgley takes another step closer to me.

"Do you want to go to the library this Saturday?" he asks.

"The library?" My heart keeps pounding in my chest so hard, I'm worried it's going to pound right out of me.

"She's not busy!" Minerva exclaims.

I stare at my sister and gather my pounding heart. Then I turn back to Ridgley. "I don't have plans," I try to say in a clear voice, but my words totally tremble.

"The one in Providence," he says. "My mom can drive us. It's awesome. The library is, like, five stories high, and every floor is a different section."

"That sounds great," I say.

"Cool," he says.

Now we both look at the floor.

At the same time, a door opens.

"Ridgley?" His mom's face peeks out from around the side. "You ready?"

"Yeah, Mom."

She smiles at me. "You must be Margaret."

"I am."

"It's nice to meet you. I'm Diana."

"It's nice to meet you," I say.

Ridgley turns to leave, but before he goes, he turns back to face me. "I'm excited for Saturday."

"At the library," I say.

Then Ridgley heads out the door with his mom.

"Kissy, kissy." Minerva puckers her lips.

"Cut it out," I say like I'm annoyed. But really I feel

great. So great that I'm not ready when I remember Dad. My brain turns like the flip of a light switch.

"Do you think he's waiting for us?"

"What do you mean?" Minerva says. "He wants to go to the library with you! Of course he's going to wait for you."

"Not Ridgley. Dad."

Minerva says, "Oh."

I go from feeling happy to sad so quickly that it takes my breath away.

"He was at the game," I whisper.

"I saw him," she says. Then she shakes her head. "He's got to figure his stuff out. So does Mom. It's not that I don't care about them. I do. But they need to figure it out for themselves."

"Yeah," I say. "It's not our job."

We both get quiet as we hear people in the gym. Minerva motions toward the door. "Are you coming, or what?"

"Sure," I say. I grab her hand and head through the door because I know exactly where I want to be. I want to be with my sister. We walk side by side, about an inch apart, close enough that no one can fit between us.

Random Thought 306.875
Sometimes the beginning is the best
place to start.

random thoughts organized
by the dewey decimal system

    929.4–Names of Persons and Places

    790.2–Performing Arts

    177.3–Truth, Slander, Flattery

    612.8–Nervous System

    153.2–Formation and Association of Ideas

    920.1–Bibliographers

    574.4–Morphology

    792.8–Ballet and Modern Dance

    160–Philosophical Logic

    118–Force and Energy

    158.1–Personal Improvement and Analysis

    259–Pastoral Care of Families

    510–Mathematics

    332–Financial Economics

    781.1–Basic Principals of Music

    178–Ethics of Consumption

    809.7–Comedy

    790.2–Performing Arts

    364–Criminology

    173–Ethics of Family Relationships

    304.8–Movement of People

    131–Parapsychological and Occult Methods

    808.7–Rhetoric of Humor and Satire

519.2–Probabilities
133.8–Psychic Phenomena
823–English Fiction
571–Physiology and Related Subjects
126–The Self
362.2–Mentally Ill
117–Structure
811–American Poetry in English
612.9–Other Parts of the Body
791.6–Pageantry
302.2–Communication
306.875–Sibling Relationships

Read on for a peek at
ALEX THAYER'S

HAPPY & SAD & EVERYTHING TRUE

<u>worst advice ever</u>

When my best friend, Juniper Green, was placed in a separate sixth-grade classroom from me, my mom said, "How interesting."

She said, "Look at what the world is giving you."

She said, "This is a wonderful opportunity to make a new friend."

She said, "You lucky girl!"

To be clear: this is not interesting, wonderful, or lucky.

Which is why I'm sitting on a toilet in the sixth-grade wing of Jefferson Middle, hiding. The bathroom is empty. The air smells like bleach mixed with a peanut butter sandwich. The beige tiles, which I like to count for something to do, gleam like wet noodles. The sink faucet in the far-left corner doesn't turn off all the way. *Da-wip, da-wip, da-wip . . .*

My classmates from 6-B are having Snack and Stretch. It's a ridiculous activity, which seems obvious, given the name. Still, I'm happy to list the reasons why. First, I mean, seriously, Snack and Stretch sounds like something toddlers do. Second, seeing how Juniper is in 6-O and her Snack and Stretch happens an hour later, I've got no one to sit with. Third, it's way better to feel alone with yourself than alone in a crowd.

I grab a Sharpie from my back pocket and write in small letters on the toilet paper dispenser *dee*. It's the seventeenth time I've done this, marking my one visit per day since the start of sixth grade. Then I go back to counting the wet-noodle tiles. *One hundred and thirty-four, one hundred and thirty-five . . .*

The bathroom door squeaks open, and voices flood the room.

"Pomegranate seeds."

"That's the smell."

"Sweet—"

"Sour—"

"Come on—"

"Trust me."

The three voices cut one another off like bumper cars. I stay on the toilet, pull my feet off the floor, and clutch my legs to my chest.

"Did you know Harry Casey bites his nails? Like, he bites them so much, the tips of his fingers start to bleed. It's crazy intense."

"I saw him. He was trying to hide it, covering his mouth with his other hand."

"Oh my god, can we go back to her? That smell."

"Is cabbage a fruit?"

"Vegetable."

"Does she smell like that?"

"Totally."

"Is it true about Harry?"

"Wait, can we go back to Dee?"

"She smells. Like cabbage."

"Totally."

"That's why no one sits with her at lunch."

"You guys, it's kind of sad. Don't you know her mom? She has lot of"—the voice lowers to a whisper—"boyfriends."

"Dee?"

"Are you kidding? Her mom. Dee's super weird. Who would like her?"

"Yeah, she's gross."

My heart beats hard like it wants to push up my throat. Tears gather at the bottom of my eyes, so I pinch the bridge of my nose and look up at the tiled wall to keep from crying.

I will never cry at school. Never.

"So gross," the voices say at the same time.

After that the door squeaks open. The voices leave. As quick as a light switch, the bathroom is quiet. My sweater clings to my neck. I pull it from my skin, trying to stretch away the itchiness.

Smelly. Weird. Gross. I cover the *dee*s with my hands. My throat aches. I wish Juniper was here. She would've told those girls that they're being superficial and mean, not to mention that they overuse the word "totally." I pull my hands off the dispenser. The *dee*s are right in front of me.

<u>facts about my name</u>

I'm named after my great-aunt, who I never met, and she's dead.

One of the nicknames for my name is Dezzi.

I do not let people call me Dezzi.

"Dezzi" sounds like someone who drinks

pickle juice and listens to saxophone music.

I think my name is why my dad left. I bet he and my mom argued about it when I was a baby.

My middle name has the word "man" in it, which is weird, because I'm a girl.

Desdemona Hillman Diller.

Most people call me Dee.

After Snack and Stretch, I have PE, another subject that's terrible without Juniper. But as I turn the corner, I see tons of kids piling into the gym. 6-B and 6-O. Plus, there are seventh and eighth graders in the gym. Talk about intimidating. I keep my head down and follow the crowd into the high-walled gymnasium. Chatter echoes against the walls. The place is packed. I scan the room looking for Juniper. I don't see her anywhere.

What I do see: parents. Hold on. Parents?

Mr. Fender stands near the bleachers. He holds a cone-shaped megaphone near his face. "Okay, everyone, time to find your partner!" He points to the far end of the gym. "Find your partner and line up! Parent PE Day is about to begin!"

Parent PE Day. Oh my god. How could I forget? Parent PE Day, also known as A Total Nightmare. Please, please, please tell me my mom isn't here. Please, please, please tell me she kept her promise. Please, please, please tell me she isn't going to show up. I close my eyes, not breathing.

When I open my eyes, I see my mom standing near a basketball hoop. She's wearing a black minidress that looks more like a T-shirt than a dress. Her blond hair is pulled into a low bun, her makeup makes her look even tanner than she already was, and she smiles, showing her white, white teeth. I scan lower and see a pink-and-gold ring on her middle finger. Even lower and she's wearing . . . thigh-high boots with two-inch heels. I shake my head. She won't be able to run at all.

She hasn't spotted me yet, and a moment later I watch Mr. Fender rush over to her. When he reaches her, he lowers the megaphone. Mom smiles. He smiles back. She says something. What is she saying to Mr. Fender? I run over to them.

"Hahahahahahaha!" Mom laughs.

"Hahahahahahaha!" Mr. Fender laughs.

"Mom," I interrupt. "You said you weren't coming."

"Darling! I thought I'd surprise you! Surprise! Your

teacher was just telling me . . . " She bats her eyes at Mr. Fender. "I'm sorry I didn't get your name. I'm Suzanne."

Mr. Fender clears his throat. "It's a pleasure to meet you, Suzanne. I'm Edward."

Edward? Mr. Fender's real name is Edward? Teachers are not supposed to have first names! I mean, I know they have first names, but they aren't supposed to use them. At school teachers need to be teachers. Mr. Fender needs to be Mr. Fender.

"The pleasure is all mine," Mom says. Then she turns to me and smiles, her teeth glistening. "Dee, darling, Edward was just telling me that you and I are going to be tied together for some sort of race."

"A three-legged race!" he adds.

Mom claps her hands. "What fun!"

ways to die
eat rat poison
crawl into bed with a snake
open emergency exit door of an airplane midflight
stand in an elephant's shadow
tie yourself to your unathletic mother and begin running

Mom looks at me. "Let's race together!"

"Uh, actually, I already promised I'd be someone else's partner. Sorry!"

I've got to find a different partner. I look for Juniper. I don't see her anywhere, but I do see Harry. He's standing near the supply closet.

Usually Harry is friendly and funny and loves to tell jokes, but he doesn't look like he wants to tell a joke right now. He also doesn't look like he wants to participate in Parent PE Day. Harry looks nervous, gnawing on his lower lip, like he'd much rather be gnawing on his nails. I remember the voices in the bathroom. They said he was biting his nails. Why were they talking about Harry? I don't know. I don't know why. Biting nails seems pretty normal to me. My attention turns back to Harry. He's standing next to a tall guy. The guy next to Harry is wearing a business suit and a frown. It must be Harry's dad.

My eyes keep searching the room until—boom. Juniper.

She's standing near the water fountain with Cordelia and Emme, two girls from 6-O. I run over to Juniper without saying goodbye to Mom or "Edward." When I get to the fountain, Cordelia is talking to Juniper. Cordelia speaks with a loud voice. She's a new student at Jefferson Middle, but you'd never know by listening to her. Cordelia is loud and a bit bossy, like she's been at this school forever.

Now Juniper is talking to Cordelia. "Yeah, both my parents are here. They'll probably race together." Juniper rolls her eyes. "They do everything together."

"At least they're here," Cordelia says. "Mine probably forgot."

"Oh, I wish mine forgot," Emme chimes in. "My dad is wearing wind pants."

"Same." I place myself in the conversation. "I mean, same, I wish my mom forgot, not same, my dad is wearing wind pants. I don't know what he wears."

Emme looks confused. I turn to Juniper, hoping she'll explain in her funny, confident way that my parents are divorced.

But Juniper scans the gym, like she didn't hear me.

It's very strange. Maybe Juniper needs to get her hearing checked? Maybe she bumped her head at camp this summer? Juniper's mom, Bernadette, signed Juniper up for, like, ten thousand camps this summer. Piano, soccer, arts and crafts, rowing . . . She was so busy, we barely got to see each other, while I spent my summer reading books, listening to records in the kitchen, and hanging out with Norman.

My mind is thinking so much about Juniper, I almost don't hear Emme ask me the following question.

"So, your dad doesn't live with you?"

I want Juniper to explain to Emme that my dad left when I was a little kid. Juniper is very good at talking to people and making them feel comfortable. But Juniper stays quiet.

I take a deep breath and say in a jumbled rush of words, "Nope, my dad doesn't live with us. I don't remember him ever living with us, but I guess he did. At least that's what my mom says. But I don't know much about him. We do have this juicer named Esther, and I wonder if my dad gave Esther her name. I think it's a funny name, and it doesn't sound like a name my mom would've thought of."

I stop talking. They all stare at me, like I've said the wrong thing, like I just gave them way too much information.

So I quickly add, "We got the juicer a long time ago."

Again, none of the girls respond. The silence is terrible. I look at Juniper, hoping she will rescue me with her words. She doesn't. She stares at her feet.

Then Emme asks, "So you live with your mom?"

"Yeah," I say.

"And your mom is at Parent PE Day?" Emme says.

"Unfortunately, yes." I motion toward my mom. "She wants to be my partner in the race," I say. "There's no way she can run in those boots." I turn to Juniper. "Will you please be my partner?"

Juniper pauses. She never paused when we were in the same class. I hate pauses.

"Sure," Juniper says. "I'll be your partner, Dee."

Cordelia nudges Emme. "You're my partner."

"Totally."

"What about your mom?" Juniper asks me. "Who will she race with?"

Cordelia cuts in. "Looks like she's partnered up with Mr. Fender." Everyone follows Cordelia's gaze to where Mom and Mr. Fender stand. Mr. Fender has given my mom the megaphone. Mom's fiddling with the knobs, laughing. Mr. Fender watches her and blushes.

"Weird," Cordelia says.

I look at Juniper, who looks at the floor. She doesn't say anything mean about my mom. She doesn't say anything nice, either. She keeps staring at her feet. It's completely strange, the way Juniper is acting. I really don't like how she's pretending to be somewhere else.

Cordelia is still watching Mom and Mr. Fender. She laughs.

"It's super weird," Cordelia says.

I'm too embarrassed to say anything, so I don't.

A few minutes later Juniper and I are tied at the ankles, our feet touching the white line in front of us.

"You ready?" Juniper asks me.

"Ready," I reply.

Finally things feel normal. I'm happy to be partners with Juniper. I'm happy we are tied together. I'm happy Juniper is right by my side, instead of pretending she's somewhere else.

Other sixth, seventh, and eighth graders and parents are lined up around us. Cordelia and Emme. Mom and Mr. Fender. Harry and his dad. Juniper's parents, Earl and Bernadette, who are wearing matching sweatshirts. Dozens of couples wait at the white line. More people watch from the bleachers. There's over a hundred people in the gym.

A whistle screams and the race begins. Juniper and I count our steps to keep rhythm. "One and two and one and two and . . . "

Our running sounds like music. We are way ahead of everyone. We keep going.

"One and two and one and two and . . . "

Then I hear "Oh my!" It's my mom's voice.

"Hang on, Suzanne!" Mr. Fender says.

I stop with Juniper and turn to see Mom and Mr. Fender sprawled across the floor, still tied at the ankles.

"Hahahahahahahahaha!" Mom laughs.

"Hahahahahahahaha!" Mr. Fender laughs.

Everyone in the race has now stopped and turned with their partner. Mr. Fender tries to stand and falls. Mom's dress has ridden up and wrapped itself around her waist. Everyone in the gym can see them. Her underwear, lacy with little blue flowers.

My face burns. My forehead, my cheeks, my neck. My whole entire body burns. I'm so embarrassed, it feels as though I've been set on fire, like my mom just lit a big box of matches and tossed it in my direction. I can't cool off. I can't stop sweating. I can't make the feeling go away.

I turn to Juniper, hoping she will say something to make me feel better. But Juniper won't look at me. Instead she's looking at her mom, who is frowning. My mom keeps laughing. The sound of my mom's laughter embarrasses me. It's always embarrassed me. Her laughter is loud and high-pitched and breathy. I wish she would stop.

She doesn't. Mom keeps laughing, still tied together with Mr. Fender. I wish I could evaporate. I wish my overheated body would evaporate and disappear. I look back at Juniper. She still won't look at me. After that, Juniper leans over and loosens the double knot between our feet. The rope falls away. I want to melt and hide and evaporate, tuck myself underground, and never come back to this gym.

Juniper rushes over to her parents. Juniper's dad, Earl, watches my mom and Mr. Fender. He rubs his chin as if he's very confused. Juniper's mom, Bernadette, watches my mom and Mr. Fender. She looks horrified. Her brows pinch together, and she frowns. Then she gives Juniper an enormous hug. She buries Juniper's face in her chest, protecting Juniper from the sight of my mom's underwear.

It's awful.

Even though the gym is packed, even though people are all around me, I feel completely alone. I don't think I've ever felt this alone. It would be better if I were actually alone, because feeling alone with my mom and my best friend and the entire middle school in this gym is the absolute worst. Which is exactly why I go back to the bathroom.